REDEMPTION

DARK HORIZONS 2

VALERIE TWOMBLY

Copyright © 2020 by Valerie Twombly

Cover by Original Syn

Editing by JRT Editing

ISBN - Print 978-1-7923-3937-0

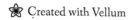 Created with Vellum

DEDICATION

For two wonderful women, Jamie, and Amy. You're more than co-workers. You are laughter, shoulders to cry on and great listeners. A safe place to vent without judgement and you don't care how many f-bombs I drop. You are women who lead by example and are some of the kindest people I know. You also love dogs which makes you awesome in my book. I'd like to think Emma carries a little of both of you in her character.

INTRODUCTION

He was promised redemption, but it wasn't what he bargained for.

Decker has everything a man could want in life. That is, until a demon named Arsenia decides to turn him into a vampire. With his life left shattered, the ex-Navy Seal is forced to make a deal with an archangel. The Red Death has spread across humanity and his new abilities are needed to help those who survive. All he has to do is complete the biggest mission of his life, then redemption will be his.

Emma was born with the gift of helping others. Her immigrant father worked hard to send her through nursing school and couldn't have been prouder when she landed a job in a big city hospital. All that is gone when the plague hits. Emma finds herself scared and alone with one tiny survivor. Rescue is a welcome relief, that is until she finds herself longing for a man who promises to break her heart.

The rule book has been tossed aside in this new world. The plague continues to change, and no one knows what the next wave will bring. Emma believes her and Decker belong together and she's willing to fight for a chance at love. However, he has no desire to travel that path again. Emma is changing and without her fated mate, she may not survive. History appears to be repeating itself, but this time Decker has a chance to alter its course. If only he can face his demons.

PROLOGUE

THE WORLD HAS BEEN SENT **into turmoil. Millions will perish and those who survive will become hope for the future. A new and very different world will emerge and this is how it all began...**

ARSENIA KEPT TO THE SHADOWS, still unsure of where she was, or even who she was anymore. The world had changed since she'd been put to sleep several centuries ago. Her father, the Inca king, had decreed she would sleep until they found a cure to save his only daughter from death. That she walked, led her to believe that day had come.

She vaguely recalled her slumber, but her resurrection was an event she would not soon forget. An angel had come and woken her and the first thing she'd done was bite him. Her mind had been filled with only one thought and that was to drink. She needed blood and his had tasted like the heavens with a tinge of darkness. There had been no time for shock at her actions to settle in. It was only after she'd sank fangs into his flesh and had her fill that she ran. Fearful of what she had done, she had gone into hiding. It had only taken her two days to recall what her mission was. The demon, who put her into stasis so long ago, had given her the vision.

Arsenia was to be reborn a vampire. An agreement she had tried to argue against, but he had said a higher power chose her. It was a vision she'd had a hard time digesting considering he was a demon. Now, she was awake and nothing could be done about it. Deep in her soul, she had a need to fulfill. The mission was crystal clear to her now and needed to be carried out without delay. Choose four prime male specimens and change them. The demon said she would know who if she followed her instinct. He'd also assured she would know how.

When asked what the purpose of this mission was, the demon replied, "The four will be the first, the primordials and they will help save the world. Or, what will be left of it." He'd laughed then refused her any more information than that. So, here she was. Clinging to the shadows and stalking prey like some wild animal and all while the prince of darkness was hot on her heels. It hadn't taken her long to figure out who he was and he was desperate to catch her and not for anything good. He would lock her away for the deeds she performed now. Of that she was certain.

Arsenia must fulfill her mission then hide. It was to be her life and she supposed she'd earned it. Exchanging death for a chance to live. The demon had never promised her resurrection would be filled with days of royal pampering. That was now a distant memory.

Heels clicking as she crossed the street, she stepped into a place called a bar. She had studied up on these social drinking establishments and found them fascinating. Thankfully, her demon had left her with the ability to adapt to the current decade. She slipped onto a stool, ordered something called a hurricane then glanced at the table in the corner.

It was her luck that the four men who sat there were who she sought. Four perfect specimens of well-defined muscle and rugged good looks that would stir any female's sexual desire. Had this been during her reign, she would have made these men her personal guards and play toys. As it were, they were the chosen. What the people here called a Navy Seal who excelled at their job. Perhaps that was why they were to be turned? She was to sire the primordials and they would sire more vampires. The order was not for her to question, only do what they had forced her into. Now that she had them in sight, it was only a matter of days before she would make them vampires like her. Like it or not, it was what they were all destined to be. She hoped what the demon had said was true, for her newly honed instincts spoke of much death to come.

The world was about to plunge into darkness.

RHEA SCANNED HER SURROUNDINGS. Since she had studied the human realm for many years, it was easy to determine they were in Peru. Aramu Muru, a sacred place where the Gate of the Gods was carved into the stone. The gate had been dead for centuries. The fact they were here now was a distressing sign.

"By the time anyone discovers you—if they can even get near the place—it will be too late. If you should survive this, I'll be back. I have big plans for you, so make sure you do survive." Her captor laughed, and she wished for a blade to gut him.

She would survive, and she would get free. She was an angel, created by the hand of the Almighty himself. That had to count for something. Right?

Mark pulled the cuffs from her wrists. She tried to plant her fist on his jaw, but was too weak, and he was stronger than before. With a snap, he broke her arm, but she refused to cry out and give him the satisfaction of knowing he hurt her. Instead, she spit in his face.

"Fuck you." Was her soul now tainted from the hatred she felt?

"Oh I intend to do that too. You just hold tight, sweetheart, and I'll be back for you. Then I plan to have you every way possible." He shoved her against a wooden pole sunk into the ground and jerked her arms behind it, securing them with the cuffs. He then took a length of rope from a bag and began wrapping it around her, binding her to the pole.

Sweat trickled down her temple as the pain of her broken limb caused her vision to skew. Rhea refused to succumb. She drew on years of training and sheer determination and shook the fog free. She had to be strong for the child she carried inside her. Certainty that her son still lived was her driving force.

Mark ripped the front of the red gown she wore, exposing her breasts. Producing a knife, he began to carve symbols on her chest. Biting her lip, she tried to draw strength from the pain. Words in ancient Latin spilled from his mouth and when she realized what he was saying... What the symbols were...

"No!" she cried out.

There was no stopping it. When he'd finished carving three symbols into her skin, and her blood welled to the surface, trickling down her belly, he stepped back. When the last word was uttered, a flash of white light filled the gate. A rumble shook the ground beneath her and suddenly the gate opened, filled with swirling blackness. The box Mark had set a few feet away exploded, and in its place stood the one man who had set this catastrophic event in motion.

Lucifer.

Rhea struggled to free herself, but it was useless. She was already weak and grew more so as her blood coated the fabric of her dress.

Lucifer raised his arms into the air and shouted. The words he spoke were a language so old she wasn't sure she interpreted it correctly. One thing was certain, he now owned the Gate of the Gods, and she watched in sheer horror as demons stepped through. Not just any demons, but the dregs of Lulerain.

No, no, no!

Lucifer had opened his gate directly to the pits of Hell, and now the worst of the absolute worst of evil spilled from its doorway. When Rhea thought it could get no worse, the most gorgeous man she had ever laid eyes on filled the gateway with his muscular form. His long raven hair lifted in the breeze, and his golden eyes surveyed the area with that of a predator before they landed on her. Her heart nearly stopped.

"Morbus," she whispered. Latin for disease, he was aptly named.

Humanity was about to face its biggest test ever and millions would perish.

CHAPTER ONE

CURRENT TIME...

DECKER SNARLED as the exposed skin on the back of his hand blackened and the stench of burnt flesh reached his sensitive nose. "I fucking hate this plague."

"Hang tight, Kayla's opening a portal to get us back to the compound," Ryder replied.

Thank god for Ryder's mate, she'd somehow gained the gift of whomever her demon ancestors were and was able to open portals. A real handy thing, especially since they'd gone on a scouting mission last night that ended with them fighting rogue vampires and a few demons. It had kept their small party of ten occupied and outside until the sun began to rise. He tried not to look up at the blasted ball of fire that he, and all the others, had now become sensitive to. So much so, that it threatened to turn them to ash. The only ones still immune to the sun's rays were humans and mated vampires. The rest of them were sitting ducks. Decker hated being a sitting duck. He'd been in control of every aspect of his life up until he'd been turned into a blood-drinking predator by Arsenia. If he ever found that she-devil, he was going to rip her head off.

She'd cost him everything.

The sun's rays cast a shadow under the only tree they had available until Kayla showed up. Decker had three of his vampires out here, as well as two of Ryder's. The shade wouldn't fit all the hulking men so Decker stepped out and fully exposed himself so the others could use the shelter of the tree.

"What the hell are you doing?" Ryder shouted. He was a mated vampire and therefore immune to the newest round of the plague or whatever you wanted to call this shit.

"Giving the others a chance."

"You're a stupid fuck."

"I'm primordial. It will take me longer to die than our men." He was not only a primordial—the first and only of Arsenia's vampires—like Ryder, but Decker was Arsenia's very first vampire. He was stronger than any of them and it was going to take a lot more than a few burns to bring him down. He tried not to flinch as his skin blistered and he wished for a hooded jacket instead of the sweatshirt he wore. It was a stupid move, but he hadn't expected to get stuck outside when dawn came. It was a mistake he'd not be making again, that was for certain. He swore under his breath that if he found Arsenia, he was going to drive a stake into her heart *then* rip her head off. He'd make sure that bitch didn't rise again.

The air shifted and magic crawled across his skin, indicating Kayla had opened the portal. Thank god for some small favors.

"You men first," he commanded to the other vampires huddled in the small amount of shade they had left. None of them hesitated and jumped into the spinning vortex of inky blackness dotted with pinpoints of white light. Once all the vampires were through, Decker sent the humans in next even though Ryder tried to argue that Decker needed to go now. His friend should know better. They'd both commanded missions as Navy Seals in their human life and never would either of them go into safety before their team was secure.

When it was only Decker and Ryder, Ryder gave him a shove.

"Get the fuck out."

This time he didn't argue but stepped into the portal and was pulled through a funnel of darkness back to the compound. On the other side, there was a commotion in the corridor as he was steered away.

"You need to come to the infirmary," a gentle voice spoke.

"I'm fine."

"Like hell."

He looked at the small, feisty female. Well, next to him she was petite, but most any woman was. "I'll heal."

She narrowed her dark brown gaze at him. "You may be commander out there, but in here when there are injured, I'm in charge. You need to feed at the very least to speed up healing."

He knew she was right, but he was a stubborn man. He also only fed when he was at absolute zero and was forced to. He hated what he'd become. Despised what it had cost him. The price had been far too high to pay. However, how could he expect his own men and the others here at the compound to obey the nurse if he refused?

"Fine." He followed her down the dimly lit corridor. Every step was filled with pain, indicating he had probably gone too long between feedings. His skin hadn't even started healing yet. Not a good sign.

"In here." She held open the door, and he entered a small exam room. "On the table, please."

He was too tired and sore to argue with her further. "You'll send one of the females?"

She shut the door. "Why? I'm right here and you need blood now."

How was he supposed to tell this woman she set his body on fire anytime she was near? His reaction to her was stronger than any of the other women he'd been feeding from. He purposely stayed away from Emma Torres because she was nothing but trouble for him. A guilty pleasure he didn't need or deserve.

"You fed anyone before?"

A brow shot up. "Seriously? We've been at site R for four months. I've fed my share of vampires." She looked him over. "I'd suggest the wrist so I don't have to get close and hurt you. Those burns look pretty bad." She stepped toward him, between his parted thighs. He inhaled, taking in her spicy aroma and was able to deconstruct it down to each component of cinnamon, clove and peach.

She held her arm out, offering him a taste of her fruit. He reached for her, brought her wrist to his nose. Yep, that was most definitely her the delicious scent was coming from. He kissed her wrist, her pulse beat hard beneath his lips and it beckoned him in so many ways. Fangs filled his mouth, and he pressed them to her skin yet didn't puncture through. He held back, liking the small gasp that escaped her lips. Her eyes closed, and she tilted her head back slightly, allowing her dark mass of curls to fall around her shoulders. She was an erotic picture even fully clothed and visions of her naked flesh filled his head.

He bit.

A mixture of sweet and spice touched his tongue then slid down his throat as he swallowed. Her blood was potent as his wounds were already starting to heal. As he looked at her, he noted the slim column of her neck and vowed the next time he drank from this beauty, it would be from that vein.

You can't drink from her ever again. If he did, he might lose all control.

SHE KNEW HE WATCHED HER, but there was no way for Emma to stop her moans. Feeding the vampires always proved pleasurable, something that had surprised her even though she'd heard the rumors. For some reason, however, feeding this vampire caused every nerve to become hypersensitive. Every touch brought heightened sensations that were near electric. She was grateful he was tapping the wrist and not her neck. Having his tongue against such a sensitive part of her skin, then his fangs piercing her flesh might be her undoing. Yes, she was certain it would cause the heat that now resided at her sex to engulf her and she might actually beg him for something she'd dreamed about the entire time they'd been at this compound.

Being the only nurse here, Emma had seen her share of well defined, naked flesh. Vampires were exceptional creatures. She wasn't sure if it was because all of them had been in tip-top shape in their human life or if it was a change their body went through when they were turned. Either way, the vampires were like supreme athletes on some kind of super steroid. Excellent vision, heightened reflexes and superior speed. They were both frightening and fascinating. Decker was one that had caught her eye. Aloof, he rarely spoke more than a few words to her during the exams she performed. She understood that like Ryder—the vampire who had rescued her—Decker was an elite Navy Seal who had been one of four turned by a demon named Arsenia. She didn't know any more than that.

Her focus came back to the sensations that filled her body. They were far more electric than with any other vampire she'd fed, and if he didn't stop, she was going to explode. Panic tried to override the impending climax. Never had she gone this far while feeding one of the men. The pleasure it usually brought her was more of a feeling of euphoria, but never an orgasm. To allow such an intimate thing to happen with Decker was out of the question. She couldn't expose that part of herself so she opened her eyes and looked at him. He was healed so why did he continue to feed? There was no mistaking the erection that pressed impressively against his jeans. Did he do this for his own pleasure? If he thought for one minute she was going to ask him for sex, then he had—

Damn it! Her nipples hardened and pressed against the tee she wore, exposing the fact she had on no bra as well as her arousal. The throbbing at her sex matched every pull he took from her vein. Intensified with each one. The sensations that rocketed through her were not going to stop until it consumed her entire body. The buildup was near brutal in force, and unlike anything she'd experienced before. There was no stopping it as it consumed her, and the last thing she saw before she slammed her eyes closed and allowed it to devour her, was the intensity of his blue eyes staring back at her. They held a hunger that both scared her yet tempted her for more. Her entire being floated with an almost out-of-body experience as she cried out so loud, she was certain the entire compound heard her. She was no longer the master of control because he had shattered it.

With another cry, she tore away from him. Blood gushing from the still open puncture.

"Why did you do that? You're still bleeding." He reached for her, but she slapped her palm over the wound and took a step back.

"You had no right." She snarled, not recognizing her own voice. Her body was still racked with after-effects of the climax.

He offered a lopsided grin. "While I'm flattered you think I did that intentionally, I can assure you that was your body's doing. Not mine." Then his brows slashed down. "Now, allow me to close that before you bleed out." This time he grabbed her arm, and there was no fighting him. He made a couple of quick swipes with his tongue, and the wound closed.

"It would have clotted."

"It would have scarred as well. I could never allow that to happen." He studied her. "Gaining pleasure from feeding us is no reason to be ashamed. Are you saying I'm the only one to bring you to orgasm?"

Just the word orgasm from his mouth caused her face to heat. It was ridiculous, she was a grown-ass woman and one who had gone to nursing school. She was past being embarrassed. "First off, it's none of your business. Second, you were healed, therefore had no reason to continue feeding except to torment me."

This time he let out a laugh. "If that was torment, then I would willingly pay to see your pleasure." He looked over his healed flesh. "Perhaps I could have stopped sooner, but you were such a delightful sight. I wanted to watch you come undone."

She slapped him, positive her hand stung more than his cheek. "I'm not your amusement. Now, get the fuck out of my exam room."

He gave an exaggerated bow along with another grin. "As you wish." Then he was gone, and she was left standing alone, trembling. How would she ever face him again?

DECKER WALKED THE CORRIDOR, still heady from Emma's blood and the scent of her orgasm. Since he'd been here for the past four months, he'd not bore witness to a more beautiful sight. There had been other females who enjoyed his bite, but none had caused such discomfort behind his zipper. His erection still a throbbing ache, he headed for his room to shower before meeting up with Ryder.

He entered the small apartment given to him when he'd been found and basically rescued by Ryder and his team back in November. The apartment was modest, but belonged to him alone, unlike many of the others on site who shared the larger bunk rooms at the compound. Stripping as he went, he turned on the shower and stepped under the warm spray. Once they left this place, it was likely there would be no more hot showers. While Decker liked the luxuries site R afforded them, he knew they had to leave. His mission was to get everyone together and up their chances of survival. After that, it would be time to collect what was promised him.

One step closer to redemption.

He tried to scrub the scent of Emma from his skin. He'd not had sex since his wife. Hadn't been able to bring himself to get intimate with a woman. Not when the painful memories and guilt ripped him apart on a daily basis. He slammed those memories into a part of his mind that he could build a wall around to protect them. The only reason they spilled forth now was because of Emma. She had been the first woman since Sophie who had even aroused him.

Was this a step closer to living again? He couldn't do it. Didn't deserve any kind of pleasure.

His beautiful Sophie. He remembered how she had glowed, her belly swollen with their first daughter. She'd been so happy. They both had been, but then Arsenia had changed all of that. The look of sheer terror on the face of the woman he loved most crept back into his memories.

He shook them away and refused to give them life. He was dead inside, and that's how he would remain. It was what he required in order to keep living. Numbness had become his best friend.

CHAPTER TWO

EMMA LEANED against the wall long after Decker exited the room. She was angry at herself for so many reasons. Her body betrayed her, and she had been within inches of giving it what it wanted. She was also mad that she had struck him. This wasn't how she acted. Not how her parents had raised her, but apparently, he brought out something inside her and she didn't like it.

She slid down the wall until her ass hit the floor. So many emotions that she'd held back for months slammed into her. The losses weighed heavily until she found herself racked with tears. She missed her parents. They had both worked so hard to give Emma a better life. Made sure they could afford to send her to nursing school. Her father worked two jobs so his daughter could have what he never could.

Now, she had nothing left of them. No photo, not a single possession. She had memories though and no one could take those away from her. She recalled how her father read to her every night. His accent rich as he read the words in English and then again in Spanish so he could teach his daughter to be fluent in both languages made her smile. Her mother would be nearby doing some chore and would whisper the words as she also tried to learn her husband's native language.

The memory faded, and she pulled herself together. Life had changed. People were dead, and it was all because of a plague. What started as a common cold by day three turned into a fever, sore throat and open sores oozing green pus. By day seven, you either survived or your heart exploded, literally. Burst open like a swollen tick filled with too much blood. As far as they knew, the only survivors of the aptly named Red Death were those who held angel or demon DNA. Or were vampire. The primordials and those they then sired—turned—seemed immune to the original plague, but the sun allergy was now a fresh round of hell that appeared to hit only non-mated vampires. Their small piece of the world was filled with demons and what they referred to as rogue vampires. Some lifeless creatures created by Lucifer, they suspected. It was more than she could take on most days, but not today.

She needed to be ready to attend a meeting the leaders planned for later in the day. There had been talk about going into town. The walk was several miles and estimated to take a good hour to get there for those still human. Vampires, of course, traveled faster when alone. They could take one of the vehicles, but Ryder wanted to conserve fuel for when they really needed them. That made sense. The weather had broken and was hitting the low forties during the day. Snow had started to melt, so it was the perfect time to venture out. Except for the damn demons and rogue vampires that showed up on occasion to torment them. Could they never catch a break?

Standing, she adjusted her clothing and opened the door. Peeking out, there was no activity, so she stepped into the corridor. As she headed for the large conference room, she wondered how she was going to face Decker.

Suck it up, Emma. You've faced far worse in your thirty-two years on this earth. Decker is a cake walk.

Right. So, she held her head high as she pushed open the door and stepped into the den of wolves. She could do anything.

"What are you doing here?"

Her gaze met a pair of ice cold, blue eyes. Decker was freshly showered. His short, dark blond hair still damp and tousled into a spiky mess. He had on fresh clothes while she still bore the same ones she'd had on when they were together. Suddenly, she felt small. A speck in the room full of vampires. Not even Kayla was here, at least not yet. Somehow Emma managed a voice.

"I've come because I'm going to town with you."

His brows arched so high she feared he might actually lose them.

"You are too valuable here so the answer is no."

Well, looked like it was time to introduce this vampire to her stubborn side. She marched further into the room and took a seat. "I don't answer to you. I'm the only medical person here. What if you come across someone who needs help? I can also look for any medical supplies."

"My men are capable or did you forget that many of us are military trained?" he responded.

"I understand that, but I'm going and you can't stop me." She crossed her arms for effect, or maybe to hide her hardening nipples. Looking at him did funny things to her body, and she hated it. "Besides, I've been through the mandatory training."

Anyone in the compound who had no weapons or fighting skills had gone through extensive training. After all, they had former Navy Seals on the team and who better to teach them how to not only fight, but protect themselves. Emma had tossed her fair share of men to the ground during training. Thankfully, Decker hadn't been one of them.

"We can discuss this later. Meantime, you can sit in on the meeting."

She offered a look that said there would be no more discussion on the matter. Granted, she had to get out the front door which was guarded, but she had her ways. For now, she'd sit quietly and listen to what the team planned.

DECKER TRIED NOT to focus on the female who had been at his mercy only a few hours ago. Her taste still sat on his lips, and her moans of pleasure filled his memories. For the first time since his wife, he contemplated scratching the itch that once again pressed against his jeans.

"Ryder, you have the map of Fairfield?" Decker brought himself back to the task at hand and the others sitting in the war room.

"Yep." The other vampire spread out a map of the entire complex and the neighboring town. Fairfield wasn't or, at least, hadn't been any larger than about five hundred people. "Not much there."

Decker sighed then looked at Ethan, the geek who'd been left behind to keep site R running. "Where is the closest hospital?"

"Gettysburg, about fourteen miles."

"Shit, that's about what—" Ryder rubbed his chin. "Five-hour walk for the best of men?"

Decker looked at Emma and knew there was no way she was staying behind should they decide to go in that direction. "At least, since nurse Florence here insists on going."

She glared daggers at him but didn't utter a word.

"We don't have the kind of daylight needed to make the trip there and back and still scout out the city," Liam offered.

"Nor nightfall," Ace countered. The only ones who could travel in the light were humans or mated vamps. What a damper that put on everything.

Decker slammed his fist on the table. "We're fucked no matter what we do."

"Well, we need to do something because the generators running this place are acting up." Ethan's jaw hardened.

"What exactly does that mean?" Decker put his focus on the man who knew more about this place than anyone.

"Look, the government cut funds. This place was supposed to get an update, but it never happened. We're okay for now, but I can't promise we won't have equipment issues."

Decker pinched the bridge of his nose. "It's always fucking something." Looking at Ryder, he said, "We're Seals, we can figure this out." They'd worked with a lot less in not so welcoming environments.

"Can't Kayla open a portal?" Emma interrupted their thoughts.

"She can, but only a small team can go through. She's still not strong enough to keep it open for a long period."

"And Tara hasn't shown any power in that department yet?" Decker asked.

"Nothing. Not even shifted." Emma had kept a close eye on the other mated female in the group. Since Kayla had been able to open portals and morph into a black jaguar, they expected Tara might also show similar gifts, but so far, nada. There was so much they didn't know about the plague, those who survived the changes. Hell, they didn't know jack shit.

Decker stared at the map again. "Ryder, what are Kayla's limits?" He hated pushing his friend's mate, but they needed every tactical advantage they could get.

"Quick moving soldiers? We can get ten through safely in one shot. If I'm there to feed her, she can reopen it at least three more times. Trouble is, after that she's toast for a good twelve hours even if I do feed her."

"So, we can move ten there and back without issue?"

"Send a scouting team ahead?" Ryder asked, then grinned. "I like where you're going. You, me, Kayla. Three of my men and the rest from your team?"

Decker nodded.

"What about me?" Emma asked.

"This is a scouting mission. You go the next time and only if we find anything in the hospital." That should keep her out of danger. They'd bring back anything of value and then there would be no reason for her to go at all.

"Not acceptable. What if there is someone out there that needs medical help? What if one of you gets injured?"

"She has a point," Ryder said, folding the map.

He didn't know why, but all of this grated on his nerves. "Fine, you can count as one of mine which means I am your commander." Let her see how she liked being treated like one of his men. "We roll out of here at eighteen hundred." He started to leave the room but stopped in front of Emma.

"We wait for no one and you better not slow down my team." He didn't wait for her response. The look she leveled at him was enough to indicate he could go fuck himself.

MMMM

EMMA PULLED ON DARK JEANS, a black, long-sleeve shirt and boots. She then tied back her mass of dark curls into a ponytail and grabbed a jacket, making sure to check the pockets for gloves. The last thing she reached for on her way from the bunks was a Navy baseball cap. It had been a find when she'd been bored one day and decided to check out the compound. Not sure if the cap had actually belonged to someone who left it behind, or was simply an extra, she decided to keep it. She liked to think if it had belonged to someone, she was keeping their memory alive in some small way.

Out in the corridor, she headed for the meeting area a good five minutes early. There was no way they were leaving her behind. Not that she was worried, she'd talked to Kayla earlier and indicated she was going as well. The other woman wouldn't allow the men to leave without her.

When she arrived at the designated area, Decker was already there with Ace and they were sorting through the arsenal of weapons.

"You need this," he said, handing her a vest.

She pulled on her jacket then donned the tactical vest, surprised at the extra weight on her body. She must have made some indication about it because Decker stared at her.

"Too heavy?"

"No. I was surprised is all."

He smirked, and she wanted to slap him again. "Good, cuz I'm not done loading you up yet." Next, he started to strap what she had learned was a Mk 23 pistol to her right thigh. The feel of his fingers through her jeans as he worked heated her skin and sent her temper into high gear. For a moment, she contemplated thumping him on the head. Why did she let him get the better of her?

"I can do that myself, you know." Her response was way too snarly, and he cocked a brow.

"I want to be sure you have this on correctly."

"Do you fondle your men as well?" Fuck a damn duck. Why couldn't she keep her mouth shut? Ace snickered, and she shot him a lethal glare.

He raised his hands in surrender. "Hey, I'm the good guy, remember?"

"I'll try to recall that in case I have to shoot something."

"I like her," he said to Decker. "She has sass."

Decker only grunted and continued on. Next, he placed three magazines in the front pocket of her vest along with a thin penlight. Would he ever stop touching her?

"That's it?" She would have thought he'd load up that front pouch.

"I like to keep the front as bulk free as possible. It makes flattening yourself to the ground easier."

Huh. Not something she would have thought of, but then again, he was the expert here. Next, he placed a radio in her left inside pouch that he connected to a coax which ran to the antenna at the back of the vest. She was beginning to look the part of a Seal herself. She just wished he would hurry up and stop touching her because she wasn't sure how much more she could handle before she started squirming.

After filling a few more pouches, then strapping an assault rifle to her, he stepped back.

"Jesus, how many weapons do I need?"

"As many as you can carry. You might not be able to kill a demon or rogue, but you can slow 'em down until one of us gets to you."

Alrighty. Another good point he made.

"Are you sure you can shoot at another life? I mean, do you have some kind of ethical bullshit that's going to keep you from pulling that trigger?" he questioned.

She hated the sarcasm in his voice. There had been a time when she would have answered yes, she would have a hard time. "I saw those bastards as they tore through our camp when we first got here. I have no problem shooting one of them."

His face lit up. "Now that's what I like to hear. You'll stay with me or one of my team at all times."

"Aren't we all going together?"

"Yes, but we'll split up once there to cover more ground."

By the time he was done instructing her, the rest of the team was there and ready to go. She only hoped they didn't encounter one of those disgusting creatures, as she really didn't want to have to use her weapons. Tonight might prove to be her ultimate test in more ways than one.

"Shall we?" Kayla asked as she used her new-found power and opened a portal. The team began moving through so it was now or never and Emma wasn't about to change her mind.

CHAPTER THREE

DECKER SENT Emma through the portal, then followed right behind her. He still didn't like the idea of her being on this mission. It wasn't a matter of her being a woman. It was more the fact she wasn't trained for this kind of stuff. Sure, everyone at the compound had been run through intensive training. They'd had nothing else to do during the long winter and he'd watched her. Knew she was capable of defending herself, but it didn't stop the bad feeling in the pit of his stomach. She might make one sexy-ass soldier, but she was a healer, not a killer. He'd have to stick to her like glue and make sure she never had to pull that trigger.

Once they were on the other side, he, Ryder and the other vampires took a quick look around. Since they had perfect night vision, anything with a heat signature would be seen. If he didn't see it, he was likely to scent it. It was one of the few things Decker found useful in being changed. That, as well as extra strength. He was nearly the perfect soldier.

"Anyone see anything?" Ryder asked.

The team responded with an all clear. The only one on their

team tonight without enhanced vision was Emma, but thankfully there was a full moon and a clear sky which should prove helpful.

"Kayla, looks like you landed us in a good spot," Decker said, pretty damn impressed. They stood outside the museum of history.

"I try my best. I guess studying the map helped." She grinned.

"All right. Let's split up and get as much done here as possible," Ryder said and took off to the north with Kayla, Ace and the rest of his team. This left Decker with Emma and his three vampires, Hunter, Nick and Carlos, who happened to be one mean son of a bitch.

"Let's go. The hospital is only a few blocks south. If we hustle, we can make it there in five." He looked at Emma. "Can you see okay?"

"Good enough to follow as long as you don't run."

"Carlos, take the lead. Hunter next, followed by Emma, myself and Nick take the rear. Don't break formation unless it's to engage." He touched Emma on the shoulder to get her attention as she was busy looking around. "If we encounter the enemy, you stay between us. Only use your weapon if necessary and for fuck's sake don't shoot one of us."

There was no way to miss the glare. If she could stab him with her eyes, he was positive she would have. He seemed to be pretty good at pissing her off.

"Do you take me for an imbecile?"

"No, I take you for a newbie and newbies always fuck up. Now let's go." He gave the hand signal, and Carlos moved out, the rest following behind him.

They made their way down the street, Decker taking mental notes of any vehicle they came across that wasn't torched or turned on its side. Some of them might still have fuel, which would be damn handy. They managed to make good time to the hospital parking lot and stopped outside the building. Decker searched for any heat signatures through the windows while Carlos and Hunter checked the perimeter. In less than three minutes, Carlos slipped into Decker's mind.

Clear back here as far as we can tell. Coming back to you.

It was damn useful that he was able to have telepathic communications with those he sired. He'd also learned—thanks to Kayla—that when he and Ryder exchanged blood, they too had the ability since they had the same sire.

Ryder, all checks out here so we're going in.

Copy that. The grocery store was already ransacked. We're moving on.

I think we'll be lucky to find much of anything here. His two men came back around and Decker gave the order to move inside.

"Emma, you tell us what floor we should hit first once we're in."

"Got it. There should be signs indicating what's where."

Carlos pushed open a door, and they filed through, rifles at the ready, all except for Emma. The stench that filtered through was unmistakable. Death hung so thick in the air, Decker tasted it.

"Ack." Emma covered her face with her sleeve but he knew it wasn't going to do a damn bit of good. Straightening, she pulled out her penlight and pointed it around the room. He hated the fact she had to use it and chance giving them away. It would be stupid to think this town was void of any life. Those fucking demons and rogue vampires seemed to be nowhere and everywhere.

"Over here," she said as she hurried to a sign. "Okay, there are two floors and a garden level. We should hit the garden level first since that's where the pharmacy and labs are." She crossed her fingers. "Let's hope there's still something left."

Carlos led the way to the stairs and carefully pushed open the door. "Fucking Christ, we got bodies." The vampire moved into the stairwell, followed by Hunter.

"Emma, we're going to switch this up. You follow me, keep your hands on my waist and I'll lead you."

"Why?"

"You don't need to see what's in there and I'd rather you don't use the light except when necessary." Never mind he was looking forward to her hands on him. Bastard that he was. "Nick, cover us."

"Got it."

Decker turned and was surprised when Emma complied with his suggestion. He figured he was going to have to pull rank and piss her off further by ordering her. When Carlos gave him an all clear, he stepped into the stairwell, enjoying the heat from her fingers as they dug into his hips. It was a shame they were in such a dismal environment instead of back at base where they might enjoy each other further. It was probably for the best, anyway. He didn't deserve a woman like Emma. Not even for one night and that was all he had to offer.

He came across a body slumped on the third step to his right. By the looks of it, the person had died not that long ago, which concerned him. That meant there were possibly people here or, at least, had been not more than a month or so ago. He sent a mental message to Ryder indicating what they'd found.

"Careful, Emma. Only a few more steps."

"There was a body, wasn't there?"

"Yes." They hit the bottom and Carlos was there holding open the door. "The body had only been there maybe a month or so."

She gasped. "That means people may still be alive."

"Don't get your hopes up. Now, which way?"

EMMA FOUGHT against retching from the smell of death. It was everywhere and blanketed her in its thick embrace. She hated it. As a nurse in the maternity ward, she was used to the scent of new life. To new beginnings. In a way, that is what was happening to them now. Lucifer had unleashed hell on earth while his Almighty father sat back and watched. According to the archangel Tegan, the Almighty had tired of humanity warring with each other and decided it was time for it to end. Hence why he didn't step in to stop Lucifer. Now, evolution was in overdrive creating new species. Had humans already become extinct? Or were they simply evolving into something else? They had learned that many humans carried angel or demon DNA, which probably saved them from this first round of the plague, but what they transformed into was a roll of the dice. Kayla was a good example. Her demon DNA had given her the ability to shift into a black jaguar. It was frightening and alluring at the same time.

"Emma?"

Decker's voice pulled her from her thoughts.

"I need light."

"Very well," he sighed. "Use your flashlight."

"This way," she stated once she had her bearings and was able to see using her light. This was one time she was envious of the vampires. They had excellent night vision, which sure as hell would come in handy right now. However, things were what they were and there was no changing it. To everyone's knowledge there were no female vampires except for Arsenia. The original who had been turned herself by Lucifer or his demons. She had no idea which and it didn't matter. Things were a mess any way you looked at it. One did have to contemplate if Arsenia had maybe done something good by turning the four primordials. It might end up being the only way some form of humanity survived.

Decker grabbed her arm and pulled her to him, his hand clamped over her mouth before she could let out a scream.

"Shhh, we're being watched," he whispered in her ear. "I want you to slowly get behind me and have your weapon ready, but we'll keep you covered."

She nodded to indicate her understanding of the situation. Decker released her, and she slipped behind him. Realized she was in the inner circle of four big vampires and freely admitted to the comfort they offered. She had no idea what was out there and couldn't see a damn thing since she'd turned off her light.

"Come out and you might survive this night," Decker commanded and Emma wondered what he was doing calling out the enemy.

She strained to see, but only pitch black and frustration met her. A shuffle, followed by a meek voice broke the night.

"Don't shoot me."

It sounded like a young girl, and Emma's hopes soared. Did they have survivors? She reached out to touch Decker. How she knew her hand had found his back and not one of the others was an odd feeling, but she simply knew. Even in the thickest of night, her gut said this was him. He'd done something to her when he had fed from her and it caused her to swallow hard. For a flash of a second, fear went through her when the word *mate* entered her head. She shook it off. There was no way in this hell or the next that she belonged to any of these vampires, let alone this one. They were way too bossy for her liking.

"Decker?"

He must have known what she was going to say because someone switched on a light. She peeked around the vampire's large frame and saw a girl covering her eyes from the light.

"Seriously? What kind of fucktard blinds an innocent girl?"

"The kind that likes to live," Decker replied, still keeping his weapon pointed at her. "So, let's start with your name."

"I don't gotta tell you jack shit. This is my place and *you're* invading my space."

Emma realized she was still holding onto Decker and a flush came over her. She snapped her hand back as if it were on fire. "Let me talk to her."

"Talk, but you're not coming out from behind me."

The girl snorted. "Does the princess need protecting?"

From Emma's observation, the girl looked to be in her late teens. Maybe twenty, but it was difficult to tell in the dark. What she did notice was the ratty mess the girl's long hair was. Her sunken cheeks and how her clothes hung on her thin frame. She was definitely in need of food and a bath.

"My name's Emma. I'm a nurse and we're here looking for any medical supplies."

"Well, Emma, you can take your hulking friends and leave. This is my place." From out of nowhere, she wielded a long blade.

"You bring a blade to a gun fight?" Decker laughed. "Not very bright."

"I'm pretty good with it and super fast." She dropped into a fighting stance. "I can take out at least a few of you before you shoot me."

"Enough of this," Decker snarled and before Emma blinked, he was across the hall and had the girl by the arm, twisting until she dropped the knife.

"Owe, you fucking prick!"

"Decker..." Emma tried to move past the team but they were an impenetrable wall. In frustration, she let out a growl and thumped one of them on the back. "Out of my way!" Somehow, she managed to slip under the outstretched arm of Hunter and make her way closer to Decker and the girl. What caused her to stop dead in her tracks was the sight that unfolded in front of her.

Without releasing his grip on the teen, he twisted his body, placing himself between Emma and apparently what he considered a threat. His fangs glistened in the small beam of light, but it was his eyes. They glowed an iridescent green rimmed with red and held the threat of a violent predator. It caused a wave of bumps across her skin, but when he spoke...

"Never. Ever. Place yourself in danger again," his voice was a low snarl as he stared her down.

She took a step back. Someone grabbed her arm and shoved her behind the fold of three towering vampires. Tucked her away from the man who now threatened his own team.

"If you ever let her out of your protection again, you will regret the consequences."

"Sorry," she muttered like a child who'd just been severely admonished.

"Whoa, you're a damn vampire!" The girl struggled against Decker's grip. "Let me go!"

"Be still. Answer my questions and no one gets hurt." He'd still not taken his focus off Emma and it did something to her. Reminded her what he was. A product of something she still didn't understand. She'd lived with vampires for several months and had grown complacent. They were all lethal and capable of killing any one of the humans there in a matter of seconds.

Emma needed to keep her perspective and remember what had happened to the world. It was no longer safe for anyone who was still human. How long before her species was gone completely?

A terrifying, high-pitched screech ripped across the room and echoed off the concrete walls. Would the terrors of their new world never end?

CHAPTER FOUR

DECKER NEVER RELEASED his grip on the girl, rather he tucked her behind him while he faced whatever now bore down on them. He sent a mental threat to his team. They now fully understood that their lives meant nothing if they allowed Emma to get so much as a scratch. He would tear their limbs off one at a time. Toss them into a pile and set them on fire while they still held enough breath to witness their own demise. He was done fucking around. Not even the seven-foot creature that stepped into view rattled him. All he wanted to do was kill it and take Emma back to the compound where he could lock her in the safety of his room.

The beast bellowed. Spread its bat-like wings to a width that filled the corridor and yet the damn things still didn't have enough room to unfurl to their full size. Red eyes were sunk into a horse-shaped head with a mouth full of razor-sharp teeth. Thick muscled arms reached out, hands tipped with three claws ready to shred anyone who came close. It stomped its hoofed foot, threatening to charge.

"Shoot that pest, then take off its head," Decker commanded.

"No!" the girl shouted and then bit Decker on the arm. The shock more than the pain caused him to loosen his hold just enough for her to twist free and run. Run straight at the beast that threatened to shred them all alive.

"What are you doing?" Carlos shouted.

"Don't hurt him." The girl folded herself into the arms of the demon. "I'll tell you whatever you want to know."

Decker was a quick study and what he saw was most certainly hard to believe. But hey, he was now a fucking vampire, so who was he to label anything as strange? "You befriended a demon?"

"My name is Tatum, and yes. He's the reason I'm alive."

Well, now this was going to prove to be an interesting story and one he couldn't wait to hear. However, they had wasted a lot of time and daylight was minutes away. He needed to send his men back with Emma to the rendezvous point with Ryder and his team.

"Here is what's going to go down. Carlos, you and the rest of the men take Emma and head out to meet up with Ryder. I'll hang back and have a chat with Tatum here."

"Deck—" Carlos began to protest but was cut off.

"Are you defying an order now?"

"No, sir."

"Decker, we're not leaving without you," Emma protested. How kind that she was now concerned about him when only moments ago she'd been frightened of him. He had not missed the fear in her eyes when he went all full vampire on her. He was responsible for her safety, and she had gone and broken her promise to follow his orders. There was no way he was having the death of another woman on his conscience. Not a fucking chance in this godforsaken hell was that happening.

"Do not disobey me again. You vowed if I allowed you to come, you would follow my orders. You failed, and now you go back. Carlos will toss you over his shoulder if that's how you want to go, but leave you will."

She opened her mouth, then promptly snapped it shut and gave him a nod. Seconds later, his team was making their way out and only the breathing of three beings filled the room.

"So, Tatum. I can't wait to hear your story."

"Fine. I lost my family to that stupid plague before we could get out of town. People died so fast..."

He didn't miss the change in her voice. The threat of her emotions spilling, but he stayed quiet and allowed her to compose herself before he spoke.

"Did you get sick too?"

"Yes, but for some reason I didn't die. Next thing I knew, I was here alone except for a few demons." She sighed. "I was out looking for food one day when I came across this guy. I heard what sounded like crying and when I went to check it out, I found him huddled behind a dumpster bleeding from a big gash in his side. I should have run, but I suddenly realized I couldn't. I felt his pain."

She flashed sorrow-filled eyes at him. "And he was scared. Much smaller than he is now. I think he was just a kid."

Decker tried to process this new information. He knew from both Kayla and Tara, who were also survivors, that they could hear demon thoughts. He remained quiet.

"So, I found supplies and patched him up. Fed him and he has protected me ever since." She shrugged. "That's pretty much it."

"Huh, your own pet demon. How sweet."

"Listen, blood sucker, you have no room to judge."

Decker, the sun's coming up and we need to open that portal now! Ryder slipped into his mind with a warning he wasn't about to heed.

Move on without me. Keep Emma safe and come back for me tonight.

Fine. Stay alive.

I intend to. The conversation ended, and he focused on the girl and her beast standing across from him. "Looks like it's just us now. My team has left for the day."

She eyed him suspiciously. "Why come at night? It's usually more dangerous."

No way was he sharing their allergy to the sunlight. He knew nothing about this girl or her demon, so he lied. "We prefer the cover of darkness."

"Huh. I guess that makes sense. Well, have fun." She covered a yawn. "Hugh and I are leaving."

"Hugh?" he laughed.

"Yeah, got a problem with that?"

"Nope. I'll just hang out here and scout out the building." He started to sweat as he watched sunlight filter in through a window. He'd need to find a dark room soon.

She stepped away from her demon and headed for an exterior door that he had somehow missed. "You shouldn't stay here."

"Why not?"

"Because this place gets overrun with all kinds of mean nasty things during the day. I don't know why."

He didn't sense she was lying. "I'm a big boy and can take care of myself."

She snorted. "No doubt, leech boy." Then she flung open the door, allowing the full strength of the rising sun to blast its way straight at him.

Fuck, this was gonna sting.

EMMA WANTED to protest more but didn't dare. She also knew it would be useless. Decker was used to having his orders followed and after the little incident, his men were not likely to let her out of their sight. Ever. They met up with Ryder and the others—Carlos filled Ryder in on the events—as Kayla opened the portal.

"Are you really going to leave him here?" she asked Ryder.

"It's what he wants. Decker is a capable soldier, even more so now," Ryder responded as he nodded for the others to start heading through the swirling mass of light. The sun was about to hit them and Emma still couldn't stop the worry that seeped through her. The vampire might have given her the best orgasm of her life then scared her half to death, but that didn't mean he should suffer. Or worse.

As she stepped through the portal, dread sat in the pit of her stomach. She should be thankful the overbearing vampire wasn't going to be there to torment and boss her. Yet, she felt empty. Funny, she should be used to that hollow feeling. It had been with her since the Red Death. Since the loss of her parents, then her co-workers one by one until she was completely alone. Emma had once thought those times during her life when people judged her, yelled at her to go back to Mexico were difficult and they were. She'd always responded that she was born in America. Never bothered to tell them she came from an interracial marriage. It was none of their damn business who her parents were. Her father had given up his country, left parents, brothers and sisters behind to make a better life for himself.

Tears filled her eyes as she made her way to her bunkroom. She missed her parents so much. Missed her life and just wanted to wake up from this nightmare. On the other side of her door, she closed it and leaned against the hard surface. The weight of her gear no longer seemed heavy to her as she pulled on the velcro straps. She let out a laugh. Never would she have thought to find herself in the position of soldier. She was a healer. Her hands had assisted in bringing new life into the world. Not taken it out.

She glanced around, hoping none of the other women she shared this room with were here to witness her breakdown. Thankfully, the room was empty, so she pulled off the vest and set it on her bed. It was time to get her shit together. Her father had taught her to hold her head high. Be proud of who she was and no matter what, love thy neighbor. Her neighbors were different now. She thought about the poor girl, Tatum. She was obviously a survivor and Emma wondered how much Tatum had lost in life. How it was she had come to befriend a beast. So many questions spun in her mind, she knew there was no use in lying down to try to catch some sleep. Instead, she finished undressing and went into the large room that held several showers and turned one on. As she washed up, she heard voices in the other room. Some girls must be back, so she lingered, hoping they might leave. She wasn't in the mood to talk to anyone right now. The only company she desired was her own.

When the voices faded, she turned off the water and dried. Wrapping a towel around herself, she walked back to her bunk and pulled clothes from the large locker next to her bed. Dressed, she wondered what to do next. The growl of her stomach said she should eat. Glancing at the clock on the wall, it told her it was already past breakfast so she would have to fend for herself. As she walked down the corridor on her way to the mess, hall she ran into Kayla.

"Hey, you doing okay?" Kayla fell into step next to her.

"I'm fine."

"It's weird that Decker wanted to stay behind."

She thought so too, considering how he had gone into full predator mode when she's tried to approach the girl. She also figured he must have given his men a mental chastising because on the way back to meet up with the others, they had not given her an inch of space and refused to speak to her.

"He seemed to want to speak more to the girl. It was really odd her befriending a demon."

"What?" Kayla gave her a wide-eyed look.

"That's right, we haven't talked since getting back. Yes, she's friends with a demon." Emma stopped at the coffee pot that was forever going. It was like there was an endless supply of the stuff and she was in need of a little jolt. God, she would kill for an iced macchiato.

"Do you know if she's a survivor?" Kayla asked.

"She is."

Kayla rummaged through the cabinets. "I'm so sick of can and boxed food. I'd give my right arm for some meat!"

"Shouldn't you be eating meat? I mean, you're a cat shifter and all." She looked at the assortment of supplies and decided she'd lost her appetite.

Kayla chewed her lip and glanced around. "Can you keep a secret?"

"Of course." Emma sipped her coffee. What she wouldn't give for real half and half. Hell, even something other than powdered milk. She thought about livestock. Cows were so domesticated she wondered if any survived. The thought of possibly seeing hundreds of dead animals made her stomach roll.

"I've gone out and hunted. Once as a cat, I caught a rabbit. I didn't want to tell anyone though."

She nodded. "I get it, People still look at you out of the corner of their eye."

Kayla laughed. "Some do, yes. They might freak out if they knew I'd hunted."

"I honestly don't know why. I mean, the men have hunted a few times. What's the damn difference?"

Kayla shrugged. "People are skittish. Can you blame them? Who knows what's going to happen next. I mean poor Tara is biting her nails waiting for something to happen to her."

Emma took another sip. "I know. Poor thing is frantic with worry most days. I've had to encourage her to try meditation to help her sleep."

"Speaking of, we should both get some."

She offered a smile. "I don't think I can sleep. Maybe I'll go practice in the shooting range."

Kayla studied her and Emma swore she was able to see right to her soul. "You're worried about Decker."

"Aren't we all? I mean, I would worry about any of us who got stuck out there." She rubbed her arms as if that would comfort her. "Every time we think we've made a step ahead, shit happens. Allergies to the sun, you shifting into a jaguar and rogue vampires?"

"Of course, you're right. It makes everything that much more of a challenge." Kayla gave her a look that said she didn't fully believe

Emma. That there was more to this than simply worrying about a fellow member of their new little society. Thankfully, she didn't say any more about it.

"Well, Ryder's waiting for me. I'll see you later." Then she left the kitchen and Emma alone with thoughts she didn't want to have.

CHAPTER FIVE

CARLOS SENT word that Emma was through the portal and safe on the other side while the morning sun washed over Decker. He waited for the usual rising smoke and searing pain, but it never came and the girl and her demon stepped outside. The door slamming behind them.

Listening to them walk away, he moved to the door. Curious, he sent caution to the wind and threw it open, stepping into the direct light. He waited, but still nothing happened. The potential reasons ran like a list through his mind. Either this was part of another change, or there was the off chance he was about to become a mated vampire. The only vampires who were immune were those that were mated. He hoped this was simply another course of the plague and the others would soon be free of their night-time bond because being bound to a female was out of the question.

Since he wasn't bursting into flames, he figured he would revisit the reason later and follow the girl to find out where she was going. Keeping his weapon drawn and his senses alert, he moved through a small courtyard. Past a pair of benches with a memorial written on them that no one would see. At least not in the near future as he was pretty sure most of humanity was gone. He then slid behind a statue of an angel whose head lay in several pieces next to it on the ground.

"Fucking angels," he muttered, thinking of Tegan and the vow he'd made. A promise that was looking like the archangel wasn't about to keep.

Decker picked up the scent of the girl and her pet demon. They were heading north, so he used his Seal training, along with his superior senses, and followed them. He stayed down wind so the demon wouldn't catch a whiff and figure out that he and the girl were being tracked.

As he moved between buildings, the full force of the sun bore down on him and he didn't even break a sweat. That his skin remained intact after catching fire recently, proved his body was once again changing. While he welcomed not being fried by daylight, he didn't like the implications.

Decker moved along the same route that he and the others had used coming in before they turned on Carlisle Street. Not once did the two he followed stop and check behind them. Instead, they continued to an open field where they headed across to what looked like a school. It would be more difficult for him to follow since there was nothing to hide behind. He'd have to wait for them to go inside before he continued. It didn't take long as the girl ran across the field while her demon pet, Hugh, trotted next to her. The entire scene was rather comical and if it were not for the fact the world had changed drastically, it would be difficult to even comprehend.

Once they vanished inside, he took off at a lightning speed run across the wet brown grass. In spots, there were still mounds of snow, but most of it had vanished and left the earth a nice mushy mess that splashed over his boots and pants. He ignored it and made his way to the brick building looming ahead. By the line of the sun, he estimated it to be about 8:00 am and still not even so much as a bead of sweat.

He tested the door and found it opened with ease. After stepping inside, his vision didn't even need to adjust to the dim light. He much preferred it. It didn't take long for him to catch the girl's scent, which he followed down a flight of stairs to the lower level of the school. There he found her in a room that held a small table with two chairs in one corner and a mattress with a sleeping bag in the other. He noticed a black, two-door cabinet, the kind you'd find in an office, on one wall and wondered what was inside.

"Where's your demon?"

Tatum screeched and jumped, plastering her back to the wall. "Fucking leech!" She clutched a knife she'd procured from somewhere.

"That can't hurt me."

She scowled. "Why did you follow me?"

He assessed from the grip on the knife she held, that her nerves were frazzled. Not to mention he scented her emotions. Another vampire trait that came in handy. While he didn't trust the girl or her demon, this was an excellent opportunity to learn more. If he gained her trust, she might tell him everything she knew and he was positive she was hiding something.

"I don't mean you any harm. I simply wanted to see how you survived and if there were any more survivors. Are there?"

"Nope."

Definite lie. He decided to offer her something. "You know, there's an entire camp of us. Survivors that is. Some vampire, some human."

The glance she cast him said the information interested her. "That's nice."

"You got this place to yourself?" He tested her again. If she lied this time, he would have to watch his back a little closer.

"Just me and Hugh."

Truth. That was a relief and he scanned the area again for the demon. Not sensing him, Decker waited to see if she offered any more information.

"You know, crossing that expansive field leaves you vulnerable to an attack."

"Hugh is always with me when I travel."

"Don't think he can't be taken out."

She glared at him. "Are you threatening him?"

"Nope, just stating a fact. Anyone with a high-power rifle can put a bullet in his head. Granted, it won't kill a demon but it sure as hell will take him down and give them a chance to get to you."

Her eyes widened. "Why are you telling me this?"

"Because you need to survive."

She seemed to accept his answer and started moving about the small room. "I suppose you blood suckers need us to stay alive so you have food."

"I won't lie. Yes, we need humans in order to stay alive but we all need each other."

"Hugh usually hunts in the mornings then comes back to guard this place," she finally offered. "Have a seat or don't. I don't care." She went to the cabinet and flung open the doors. "I'm assuming since he left me alone with you, he must trust you. Therefore, I guess I can." She eyed him. "I'm sure Hugh knew you were following us."

He wasn't so sure, but then again, he didn't know jack shit about this demon so anything was possible. As she reached for a jar of peanut butter and a bag of oats, he noted how little she had in the cabinet. Some soup, beans and a few cans of tuna.

"Do you eat food?" she asked, pouring some oats onto a plate. Grabbing a spoon, she scooped out some peanut butter and rolled it in the oats.

"A little, but mostly for taste."

"Huh. Well, I'm not feeding you, blood-sucker." She popped the spoon in her mouth and ate. He admitted, for such a young girl she seemed to do okay in her new environment.

"You can come back to our camp. We have a lot of food, other people and the woman who was with me is a nurse. If you have need of any medical attention."

She stared at him for several minutes while sucking the spoon clean. "What makes you think I need your charity?"

"It would appear you don't, but we have luxuries like heat and hot water." He didn't want to point out he thought she was way too thin.

Her eyes widened. "You have showers? How?"

"We live at site R."

She frowned. "That secret government place in the mountains?"

"That's the one." He could almost hear her gears turning as she likely contemplated a hot shower. Who knew when the last time was that she'd had one?

"I can't leave Hugh." She went back to eating her snack, her mind made up.

"You're that connected to a demon?"

"He takes care of me. Do you know he's hunted and cooked fresh meat for me?" She shook her head. "He's like the only friend I have left."

He had heard that there were good demons, but had never seen one. Perhaps this was one of those rare cases? It might be worth having Kayla try and talk to the creature. Kayla seemed able to understand demon language. "I get it. Tell me, can you talk with him telepathically?"

She snorted. "I'm not psychic."

Not a lie. So, why did she not have the same ability as the other women who survived? Did that mean she wasn't a candidate for a mate? Did that even have anything to do with it? Too many questions he wasn't able to answer and it pissed him off. He'd kill right now for someone to run DNA and bloodwork. They needed answers. There had to be someone still alive out there that could help. They just had to find them.

"Don't be offended by what I'm about to say, but if you're eating meat how are you so thin?"

"I know, I'm skin and bones. I'm not starving, but can't seem to gain weight. Not since the plague."

Another thing that didn't jive with what they knew so far about survivors. Tatum was different and they needed to figure out why.

EMMA HAD BUSIED HERSELF SHOOTING, then moved on to a rigorous workout but none of it had stopped her distress for that asshole vampire, Decker. She was so mad at him for making her worry and pissed at herself for giving a damn. She tried to blame it on her nurturing instincts. Her father had always called her his little Florence Nightingale and he was the reason she had gone to nursing school. As a child, Emma was the first to run for the bandages and wrap up her dolls. When she got older, it progressed to fixing her friends' bumps and scrapes. In high school, she volunteered to assist the nurse one day a week for extra credits and had even taken her first college course to prepare her for nursing school.

The clock on the wall told her it was dusk and Kayla would soon open a portal for Decker to return. She wondered if the young girl would come back with him. Had he found more survivors? Had he stayed out of the sun? So many questions and she found herself walking to the location where portals in and out were opened. It was almost as if she'd been in a trance and didn't even realize where she was going until she arrived.

"Emma, didn't expect to find you here," Ryder said.

"I thought I should be on standby in case Decker needed medical attention." Lame excuse and she knew it.

"Excellent idea. We are so fortunate to have you here," Ryder replied while Kayla gave her a slight grin.

She ignored them both because it was she that was lucky Ryder had found her and the baby she'd been caring for in that hospital and had brought them along. She shuddered at the thought of what would have happened to them had they not escaped. Before she could dwell more on a plight that never happened, Decker stepped out of the spinning darkness and into the corridor.

He looked at her. "I didn't expect to see you here, but glad you made it back safe." The portal snapped closed behind him.

"I don't know why everyone is making a fuss. I'm a nurse after all and always try to be here when the team comes back from rounds." She wondered who she was trying to convince with that statement.

Decker grinned. "Of course, you are, but Seals are also trained medics. Ryder could have assisted me if I'd been injured."

"Well, glad you're back. You can fill us in on the details of your findings when you're refreshed." Ryder took Kayla's hand and suddenly Emma was alone with the tall, intimidating vampire, wishing she were anywhere else.

"I sense there's something you want to say?"

She tried her damnedest to fall into a relaxed posture but this man made her body hum with sexual desire. It was distracting and the way he looked at her—like he wanted to devour her—only made matters worse. "I wanted to thank you for having my safety in mind, but the way you went about it was..." She wasn't even sure. She'd been frightened of him, yet a part of her had been intrigued by his actions. He had shown an animalistic behavior she'd never seen displayed by any of the others. She would have to remember to ask Kayla if Ryder ever acted like that.

"I told you to obey my commands." He took a step closer.

She stepped back.

"I don't tolerate any of my team doing what you did. To disobey can mean someone's life." Another step forward.

She backed up again.

"You promised to follow my orders if I allowed you to go out with us." Another step but this time she stayed put. She was done backing down from him.

"You broke your promise, and compromised all of us. Don't expect to go out with my team again."

She licked her lips. He was so close now his heat penetrated her skin until she felt a bead of sweat on her brow and her breathing became heavy. He leaned closer and she held her breath. An intense desire for him to kiss her overwhelmed her. If she were honest with herself, she wanted him.

He was close enough their lips almost met. Was he going to kiss her? She wondered what he tasted like. Would his fangs appear if they kissed? She had a naughty urge to run her tongue over one.

"Reel in your libido, Torres."

Using her last name snapped her out of her lustful haze and brought back some of her common sense. She took a step back.

"Unless you mean to fuck me." He shook his head. "I'm a temptation you don't want because all I'll be is a cock between your thighs then a cold empty spot next to you in the morning. I don't stick around for any woman. Not now, not ever again." Then he stormed away.

Emma found herself alone and shaken in the corridor. Her body no longer under her control. He'd sensed her desire which itself was embarrassing and it angered her. Angered her so much that she stormed after him, against her better judgment. It didn't take long to catch up to him and find he was still alone.

"Who the hell do you think you are?" Her voice crackled with anger.

He turned to face her and his mouth twisted in amusement. There was also an erection behind his jeans. He'd wanted her.

She gave herself a mental slap. *Remember why you're here. To give him a piece of your mind, not a piece of ass!*

"You can't expect to give off the scent of desire and not give me an erection. Or, most of the vampires in this compound right now." He rolled his fingers into fists. "Can I assume you followed me because you want to fuck?"

Damn it to hell and back again! Why was it when she was near him, her body took over for her mind? "You need to stop with the mind thing. I'm not sleeping with you." Yet, why not? That was what she wanted.

He tossed his head back and laughed. "Mind thing? I don't have that kind of power over you, sweetheart. Besides, even if I did it's not my style to force a woman into sex. I'd much rather she come to me of her own free will. Are you sure that's not what you're doing?"

Half of her wanted to punch him, the other wanted to take him up on his offer. It had been a long time—like two years at least—since she'd been with a man. His fangs buried in her was the closest thing to sex since her last boyfriend. Emma wasn't one to practice one-night stands, but she was sorely tempted. Instead, she resisted.

"You're an ass." Then she did the only thing she could, walked away.

CHAPTER SIX

DECKER LEANED AGAINST THE WALL, while Ryder sat in a chair tipped back so far it threatened to topple over. They both looked at each other while talking to Shade on the satellite phone and by the look on Ryder's face, they were both thinking the same thing.

"Did I hear you correctly?" Ryder asked for the second time.

"Asshole, I didn't stutter. Yes. The ancient ruins here in Mexico have come to life. Just like that fucking incident in Machu Picchu. Right now, it's nothing more than a swirling energy source."

"Shit, that's exactly how Machu Picchu started," Decker said, scrubbing his face. First, weird shit started happening, then the ancient people who had occupied the ruins had come back from the grave. Their king had led some angel to a chamber where his daughter, the princess, had slept for centuries. Apparently, put into some kind of stasis by Lucifer or one of his demons. Decker couldn't recall which and it didn't really fucking matter. The point was, the king had made a bargain with evil to save his daughter who had become terminally ill. No one, not even the angel who'd awakened her, knew she would become a blood sucker and turn Decker into a walking leech.

That's when shit started to go way bad, but that wasn't even the frosting on the cake. The real fallout happened when Lucifer had gotten hold of a pure angel, an angel who wasn't born but created by the Almighty himself. Lucifer used Rhea's blood to take control of and open the Gate of the Gods. He'd opened that son of a bitch straight to Lulerain, a.k.a. the pits of Hell. A place where the most foul of evil were held for an eternity of torture. A prison where Morbus had been kept. Or, otherwise known as the demon of disease. The moment that demon stepped through the gate and into the human world, humanity had been screwed.

"I don't like this," Ryder said.

"No shit," Shade replied. "I don't know what to do here. Do we try and move? Or, stay and play, see what happens? My choices aren't exactly optimal."

Shade was another primordial created by Arsenia. From what Ryder and Decker had gathered, Shade was probably the third one to be changed. It struck all of them as odd that all four of the primordials were Navy Seals. Had this been intentional? Decker didn't like how all of this felt. He never wanted this life and it had cost him a price he hadn't wanted to pay.

"Shade, only you know what's best. If the ruins near you are acting up, it's possible that's also happening other places. Or, will soon start," Decker replied. With at least two hundred in Mexico, and probably more that have yet to be uncovered, it could turn into a mess. He wondered if this was occurring at other ancient sites across the world. There was no way to know.

"Have you had contact with or found any survivors?" Ryder inquired.

"No. If any of the people here still live then they're hiding from us."

Decker twirled a pen. "How's the sunlight allergies?"

"Lost two of my vampires. Now we take extra precautions. I fucking hate this shit! I feel like we're sitting ducks. I have a hundred and forty-eight men and only fifty women. My gut says it's in our best interest to move and see if we can locate any survivors."

Ryder let out a loud sigh. "I know." He looked at Decker. "I've been thinking that maybe our best chances are if we're all together."

Decker was inclined to agree. They were in no better position at the moment. With over a hundred men combined, forty of which were vampires, they only had thirty-two women and two of them were mated and off limits. He worried about the women every second he breathed. How long could they sustain the vampires? Worse, how long before the men started to get out of line? Rape was a real fear he had and he knew Ryder had it as well. They counted on their vampires to keep the rest in check. So far, there hadn't been any issues, but they were coming. He felt the unrest and the heated stares that were cast at the women under his and Ryder's protection.

Failing them was not an option and both he and Ryder made it clear. To break their law was instant death. There would be no court system and no lawyering up to claim innocence. Decker was a walking lie detector and both he and Ryder were lethal.

"Have you spoken to Wolfe?" Ryder asked. The fourth primordial who had been heading from LA to Arizona with his people last they knew.

"No. I've tried several times to reach him but have had no success. I've thought about heading in his direction. I'm thinking of giving my vampires the choice to go or stay. I can't promise the traveling will be easy with this sunlight bullshit."

"It's a sound idea, let us know what you decide. Ryder and I need to have a talk. We'll be in touch soon."

"Take care. Until we talk again." Then Shade hung up.

"Time for a plan." Ryder walked to a map of the United States on the wall and studied it.

"Arizona is about thirty hours from here. Missouri would be about halfway. We could get to the middle of the state in about fifteen if we were traveling with just vampires. With a group as large as ours? We need to add extra time," Decker said.

"We have over a hundred souls, it's a lot of people to move."

Ryder looked at him. "We have forty vampires not counting you and me. We need to give them a choice. Everyone a choice."

"Agreed. I think it's time to bring this idea to the others. We also need to go back to town. Scavenge anything we can as far as vehicles and fuel. We need to talk to the girl too." Decker had filled Ryder in briefly about his time with the girl and her demon.

"Tatum? Yes. We need to know if there are any other survivors and give them the chance to come with us." Ryder headed for the door. "I'll have everyone in the mess hall in thirty."

THE ROOM ECHOED WITH CONVERSATION, and murmurs of the young girl discovered in town. Word had spread about her befriending a demon, and most found it to be unbelievable. Emma recalled the beast, and if the girl had indeed made friends with it, she had to hand it to Tatum. The girl probably had bigger balls than most men.

Finally, Ryder and Decker came in and took a spot at the front of the room. Everyone quieted so they could hear the reason the meeting had been called. Ryder moved forward while Decker took a seat on top of a table. Every time Emma looked at him, her skin heated and she chastised herself. She wondered if there was a store in town that had any vibrators because apparently, she needed to get herself one so she could get rid of this god-forsaken itch.

"Decker and I recently spoke with one of our teammates living in Mexico. He reported some strange happenings at the ancient ruins near his locale. He doesn't know what yet, but it sounds a lot like how Peru started and the strange energy that came from there before the ancient people came back to life."

Emma was intrigued by this information, though she didn't know why. There were mutterings in the room but no one posed a question so Ryder continued. "Shade has few people with him so he's thinking of heading out in the direction of Arizona to see if he can meet up with Wolfe and his group. That being said, Decker and I have also discussed leaving here and meeting the others halfway. Say maybe Missouri."

"Is it wise to leave here? I mean, this complex is pretty safe and we have supplies," one of the men asked.

"That's a valid point we've also discussed and we are a big group to relocate. Our concern is the number of men versus women."

"You mean the number of feeders you vampires have?" Another shouted with a little more anger than Emma thought was wise.

"That is also an issue. Everyone knew coming in what the rules were and how we needed to survive. If any of you feels this is unfair, you are welcome to leave. We won't stop you, but we also can't protect you."

Decker rose to his full height and crossed his arms. The simple act of his biceps thickening caused more heat to stir in Emma's sex.

Jesus, I might need to give up this battle and take his offer.

At that precise moment, he looked straight at her. That was not a good sign at all. Did he scent her arousal again? He looked away and spoke.

"Common sense should tell all of us that our numbers are skewed too far in one direction. Men far outnumber the women. We need to go out and see if there are any other survivors. The fact that we found one in town is a good indication that there are. Society will do far better with more people. Less chance of criminal activity too."

She knew exactly what he was referring to. At some point the threat to the women might become real. What did they really know about each other? Women's equality and all that went out the window when the Red Death took so many lives. If there ended up being more men alive than women, things would not go down well. The female gender would suffer. It wasn't far removed to think they might be forced into sexual slavery and child bearing. The thought made her shudder, and Decker looked at her again.

She had to suppress another chill that raced up her spine.

"We will travel at night, of course, but any vampires who wish to stay behind... Anyone for that matter who wants to stay here it's understandable," Ryder added. "We need to decide soon and begin preparing. More trips to town are in order before we set out."

"Can we ladies discuss this amongst ourselves?" one asked.

"Of course," Ryder responded, then he nodded to Decker and all the men filed out of the room.

A few minutes later, the women were alone, and Kayla spoke up. "I wasn't sure if you wanted me to stay or not. I'll go if you wish."

"Why would we want you to leave?" Emma asked.

"She's right, it doesn't matter that you're mated to a vampire. I mean, I know you have abilities we don't, but you're still one of us," Tara said. "None of us understand how any of this works or what might happen next. Shit, why is it you can shift and open portals and I can't do any of that?"

"Yeah, at this point, Kayla, you're the best suited among us to offer protection. I mean, all of us have been trained in combat, but it's not the same," another said.

"Thanks, you have no idea how much your acceptance means to me." She sank back into her chair. "So, what do you guys want to do? There's risk in staying and going."

"I get what Decker was trying to say. At some point it will become an issue that the men outnumber us. I trust Ryder and Decker to keep us safe, but what if something happens to one of them? I vote we leave. We need to know what's out there and how many survived."

Emma thought those were the most words Anna had said since they'd been locked up here. The woman was normally so quiet it was easy to forget she was here. "I vote we leave too. We need to locate more survivors. I have hope that they are out there and at some point, we have to rebuild." She took in a deep breath. "There's also that ticking clock. I feel it weigh on me every day. None of us are getting any younger, and the older we get the more difficult preg-nancy gets."

"God, the thought of bringing a child into this world now,"

someone said and Emma understood. It was a difficult situation they were all in.

"I know. We are going to have to play it by ear as we go. Hell, I'm not even sure I can still have kids," Kayla replied with a sigh. "Shall we vote?"

There were several murmurs of yes so Kayla brought the vote to the table.

"All in favor of leaving, raise your hand."

Emma scanned the room and counted a hand for every single woman there. "Looks like we're packing our things." She prayed they were making the right choice.

CHAPTER SEVEN

DECKER PULLED the clip from his pistol and placed it on the table. He checked the chamber then began to disassemble the weapon for cleaning when a knock came at his door. He grinned, already sensing who was on the other side.

"It's open."

The handle twisted, and Emma slipped inside, closing the door behind her. "Hi."

"Hey. What's up?" He studied her and began to memorize every curve. The way she licked her lips when nervous. He really needed to stop looking at her before he did something they'd both regret. He went back to cleaning his gun.

"So, the ladies voted and we've decided it's best for us to all leave here together."

He gave a nod. "That's a smart decision. At this point, success will be greater the higher our numbers."

"Agreed. Just promise me you and Ryder will keep your word about protecting the women."

He brought his focus back to her. "Have you had any problems I should know about?"

She shook her head. "No, and I've not heard anything from the others."

"Good. You will tell me if you do and it will be dealt with swiftly. Ryder and I, as well as those we sire, will protect you, always."

She stepped closer, a frown wrinkled her brow. "How can you know the other vampires will always follow your orders?"

He set down the cloth he'd been using to wipe the pistol and turned to face her. "Vampires are compelled to obey their sire's commands as they know what the outcome will be if they do not."

"So, say you decided to rape and pillage, then your men will obey your command to do so?" She took a step back. "You have that much power over another being?"

"If it went against their morals, they would refuse, but if I really wanted my way, I could compel them into doing my will." He stood. "Before you freak out, I appear to be the only one who can do that. Ryder and I figure it must be because I am the first of Arsenia's vampires. Second, I would only ever use that power if it were life and death for the vampire I sired." He walked to the kitchen sink and washed his hands. "I didn't rape and pillage in my human life, I'm not about to start now." He faced her as he dried his hands. "I still hold the same morals I did before."

"Of course. It was simply an analogy."

He noted she lingered as if there were something else on her mind. "Was there anything else you wished to talk about?" He moved closer to her. "I haven't fed yet, care to offer?" He wasn't even sure why he asked. He didn't need to feed, but he did want to taste her again. Wanted to feel her softness next to him as this time he would sink his fangs into her neck. No more wrists from the beautiful Emma. Her eyes widened and her arousal scented the room, but he wasn't ass enough to point out the obvious again.

They both needed a good fuck.

"Do you require it?"

Did he lie? It wasn't his nature. "No."

"Okay, then I should be going. I have some things I need to take care of." She headed for the door but stopped with her hand on the handle. Several seconds ticked by before she looked over her shoulder at him.

"I..."

"Just say what you want, Emma. I'm not here to judge you."

Her breaths increased, and he noticed her pulse beat in her neck. It did little to deflate his growing erection. When he thought she might leave, she turned completely and faced him.

"The thing you said earlier?"

He waited. "Which thing is that? You need to be specific so I don't misunderstand."

She licked her lips and looked him straight in the eyes. "The thing about us having sex."

He dared not move for fear he'd scare her off. "I recall telling you that I don't stick around."

"Yes, what if I said I didn't care?"

This time he did take a step closer. She held her ground. Good sign.

"Are you asking me to fuck you, Emma?" He held his breath.

"Yes," her voice was barely a whisper.

"You're certain?" He took another step.

"I'm certain. I know you must sense my arousal like you did before." This time she moved toward him. "It's been forever. I'm not asking for anything from you except one night. Be with me for one night and in the morning you can go."

"What if it's my quarters we spend tonight in?"

"Then I will go in the morning." She took another step, and he admired her courage. Little did she realize the danger she was playing with.

He was no longer human. Didn't fully understood himself what he was, but he knew he was deadly. "I agree with your request." He also knew there was a chance he might become inflicted with the mating mark like Ryder, but he'd drank from her and nothing more than one hell of an erection had occurred. He felt confident he and Emma were not a match.

"I ask one thing in return."

She tilted her head. "What's that?"

"Surrender yourself to me completely." When fear filled her eyes, he quickly continued. "I swear not to hurt you and you can stop at any time. I'm simply asking for you to let go and allow me to make you feel like a woman again."

SURRENDER TO THIS MAN? Emma had a moment of fear, but trusted him once he reassured her. What was it like to feel like a woman? It had been so long and with the world outside left in god knows what state, she liked his words. Liked them a lot. Why not forget themselves for this brief time? Soon they'd be heading into Hell, of that she was certain, and this opportunity may never come again.

She moved closer until they stood only inches apart. "Yes. I agree. Do you have protection?" They still had to be careful as neither knew if pregnancy was possible.

"I do." Then before she was able to utter another word, he pulled her close. Freed her hair from the tie she had holding it back and her curls fell over her shoulders.

"I like your hair. You're a beautiful woman, Emma."

"Thank you." She couldn't believe she was actually going to do this. But there was no one left to judge her, and she had an ache that was much more than sexual. She needed to have human contact. Wanted strong arms to hold her and make her forget how much life had changed. How much they had all lost. No other man here came close to stirring up the feelings that Decker did in her.

He slid his fingers along her cheek as he slipped them into her hair and bent closer. His breath heated her face, and then his lips touched hers. Gentle and brief before he pulled back slightly.

"It has been a long time for me," he whispered.

"Me too."

"Then we both need this." He claimed her mouth with such hunger her knees buckled yet she managed to stay upright.

God, the man could kiss and the fire between her thighs shot up several degrees. With every swipe of his tongue, it pushed her closer to the edge until she swore kissing him alone might send her over the cliff and into sweet bliss. There was no question now if she was able to surrender to him. Only if she could find happiness in the moments they had to share.

Emma moaned and slid her hands up his chest, disappointed a shirt covered the perfect abs she'd seen every time she had examined him. She'd spent time studying the tattoos that covered his chest and spiraled down his arms, but now she wanted to trace her fingers over the ink. She tugged at his shirt, wanting to free it from his jeans so she could fulfill her desire. He broke the kiss and grabbed the shirt, practically ripping it from his body, then tossed it aside.

"Better?"

She noticed a hint of fang when he spoke and wondered if she could get any more turned on. "Much." She leaned in and kissed his chest, liking the feel of firm muscle beneath her lips. "You can feed if you want." She glanced up and saw him grin.

"Oh I intend to, but only when I'm balls deep inside you."

Jesus save her, as she didn't think she was going to survive tonight. "I'm not sure how long I can wait." She fumbled with his belt buckle when he touched her hand.

"One thing about being a vampire, I can go as many times as you want. Seems to be a benefit, I'm told." He undid the belt and next thing she knew his jeans were gone and the thickest erection she'd ever laid eyes on was right there for her to touch.

Emma had never been shy when it came to sex, but with Decker he left her feeling vulnerable. His body was utter perfection. Hard ridges of muscle that reminded her of a sleek, powerful predator.

"You're still dressed." He broke into her thoughts, and she glanced into dark blue depths of desire.

"I guess I was busy admiring you." She smiled, then grabbed the hem of her shirt and pulled it over her naked breasts. She only wore her bra when outside on rounds. With only one to her name, it was saved for necessity only. She'd hardly dropped the tee when his mouth wrapped around her nipple and sucked. She arched into him, the sensation of his tongue swirling over her bud hardened it further. She slipped her fingers into his hair.

"Decker," she whimpered.

He cupped her ass and lifted her, carrying her across the room and into the bedroom where he laid her on the bed. He was quick to loosen her jeans and free them from her body along with her panties.

She was at his mercy.

"You are perfect."

Heat brushed her cheeks as he continued to devour her with his gaze. Then he kissed between her breasts. Made his way down her stomach until he was at the apex of her sex where he slid his thumbs through her folds, opening her. The sensations strummed her body until she feared death might occur from arousal. Was that possible?

Heated breath whispered across her core as his mouth closed in on her. A slow swipe of his tongue took her another step closer to bliss, and then something happened. He was off the bed, dressing and shouting commands. It took Emma several seconds to realize the compound's alarm was blaring, indicating rogue vampires had breached their defenses.

"Emma, up and dress. Now!"

She rolled off the bed, her legs nothing more than rubber as her feet hit the floor. She grabbed the side of the bed and braced herself while Decker tossed clothes at her. How did he dress so fast?

"Hurry, I'll grab weapons." Then he was out of the room while she tried to clear her lust-ridden mind and dress.

She swore, somehow managing to dress and met him in the other room where he already had a pistol loaded that he shoved at her. He then strapped a blade to her right thigh. "You with me?"

She nodded. "Yes." No, not really. She wanted to kill whoever dared set off the alarm and interrupt them.

"Good. Ryder says there's a breech in the women's barracks."

He must have been talking to Ryder using that mind thing the two of them sometimes did. It certainly came in handy at times like this. He cracked open the door and peered out.

"Clear. You're going to have to cover my back until we meet up with Ace, who happens to be the closest."

"Got it." Her pulse raced, but not for the reason she wanted as they entered the corridor. The lights had dimmed and flashed a red warning that sent shadows creeping along the wall.

"Stay close to me. I'll sense anyone before you see them."

"Okay." She swallowed down fear and despised the taste of it. She hated the rogues and fighting even more. It was a way of life now. They couldn't expect any peace as long as they stayed here. But would they get it if they left?

As they neared the area where the rogues had infiltrated, screams from the women ripped through the air and sent Emma's already shattered nerves on edge. She kept the pistol firmly in her grip like she'd been taught as she tried to focus in the dim light. Vampire night vision would be handy right about now.

A rogue jumped in front of them and fired a gun. Decker covered her as a spray of bullets flew through the air.

"When did these fuckers start carrying weapons?" he snarled, and she was relieved the bullets must have missed him. He fired his own weapon and as soon as the rogue vampire was down, he rushed over to twist its neck.

More screams filled the air and Emma ran toward the commotion. As she rushed into the room, thick arms reached out and grabbed her. She tried to turn into him, but was held firm. This didn't smell like Decker and when pain ripped across her neck, she realized her fatal error in leaving his protection.

"Emma!" Decker yelled.

As she looked at Decker, she noted the blood that soaked his shirt. He had been hit. She needed to get to him but couldn't move. The pain at her neck throbbed and spots flashed in her eyes. Decker faded in and out of her focus, but not before she saw a fury on his face that frightened her. His fangs glistened in the dim light. An animal growled from somewhere and then Decker was nothing more than a dark flash.

Her body grew heavy and then she was floating.

CHAPTER EIGHT

EMMA FLEW ACROSS THE CORRIDOR, her body hitting the concrete wall before she slid down into a limp form on the floor. Blood ran from the wound on her neck and pooled beneath her.

A red haze filtered across Decker's vision as he moved faster than he ever had before. He had the rogue in his grip and tore his head clean off his body. The bastard didn't even have the fucking decency to put up a fight. After tossing the body aside, he started for Emma but was pulled into another fight. His boots slipped in pooled blood, the floor slick with it, but it didn't ruin his aim as he shot another rogue between the eyes. He made quick work of breaking its neck to end this damn misery. At least two females laid at twisted angles on the floor. His keen senses told him they were already lost to them so he searched for more rogues to slaughter.

A giant black cat launched itself into the air and took out two more rogues. Kayla must have shifted into her jaguar. The changes many of them went through were proving beneficial in this new world. It looked to be the only way to survive.

Gun shots filled the air and this time a demon came at him.

"Mother fuck, I'm sick of this shit!" He launched himself at the beast and latched onto a horn protruding from its bulbous head then sank his fangs into the demon's neck and tore at flesh and muscle. The vilest taste filled his mouth, and he spat the demon's own blood in the creature's eyes. It screeched, the sound grating on his nerves until it caused a sharp pain in his head. The beast bucked and tried to loosen Decker's grip, but he wrapped his legs around the demon's thick waist while he reached for the knife strapped to his thigh. His fingers gripped the wooden handle and the moment he jerked it free of its sheath, the fucker bucked and swirled, causing Decker to lose his grip on the blade.

Steel clattered to the floor and skated before it stopped in a pool of blood.

"I'm fucking tired of you," he shouted. He needed to dispose of the demon and check on Emma. He could still see her crumpled body on the floor and she wasn't moving. If someone didn't get to her soon, she was going to bleed to death.

Gathering every reserve of strength he had, he reached for the other horn and started to twist the demon's head. The creature's neck was so thick he was having difficulty ripping the disgusting thing off.

"Decker, heads up!" Ryder shouted, and he glanced in the direction of his friend's voice.

Ryder held Decker's blade and tossed it. Sharp pointed steel spun end on end and Decker shot out his hand to catch it right before it landed between his eyes. With a firm grip on his knife, he shoved it into the demon's neck. The creature roared, sending a blast of sound that made his ears ring and his gut roll. The throbbing in his head became so intense his sight filled with pinpricks of light.

"What kind of fucking demon are you?" he grunted and then the creature sank claws into his thigh, peeling him from his position and tossed him like a rag doll against the wall. His back slammed hard enough to knock the air from his lungs as he slid to the floor. Through his blurred vision, he watched the beast open a portal and disappear along with Decker's blade still stuck in its neck.

"Bastard. I loved that knife."

Ryder stood over him, extending his hand, and Decker accepted the help to his feet. It had been a tough fight.

"I've never seen that thing before, but it's caterwauling seems to have an effect on us. I felt that shit right down to my bones and I don't fucking like it one damn bit," Ryder said.

"Emma?" He noticed she was no longer lying on the floor.

"Taken to the infirmary by Ace. He and Kayla are taking care of her, but you might want to go. I'll clean up here. We'll burn the dead at nightfall."

Decker was back on his feet. "How the hell do we fight that?"

"No idea."

"What's our status?" he asked, shoving a hand over a bleeding gunshot wound in his abdomen as he started in the direction of the infirmary.

"Three women dead and one missing. Two men dead as well and a few of our vampires injured, but they should heal. That was intense."

Decker wiped blood from his face with his free hand. "The child?"

"Unharmed."

Relief swept over him. He didn't think anyone would survive the loss of Faith. That baby was the beacon in their bleak future. "We need to get the hell out of here and soon," he called over his shoulder as he jogged down the corridor, his body protesting. From his assessment, he had three bullets lodged in his chest and abdomen along with a shredded thigh thanks to that damn demon. He'd survive. His body would expel the bullets, and his wounds would knit back together. Feeding would heal him faster, but the need to check on Emma overrode everything else.

He shoved open the door to the infirmary. The room bustled with his and Ryder's men helping patch up the injured. Thank god for medic training since their only nurse was now down. He moved along exam tables and cots, following his sense of smell until he located Emma in a private room. When he opened the door, what he saw caused him to snarl.

Ace was bleeding from his wrist into Emma's mouth.

"She's going to die," Ace said. His voice had never been so quiet. "I'm hoping my blood will help her heal." He looked at Decker. "You're a mess."

"Don't worry about me," he growled and moved closer. That's when he noticed the gash on her neck. It was far more than a bite. The fucking rogue had torn her throat. Ace made the right call. There was no way to heal from a wound like that.

"We don't know if she will change," Kayla offered, her eyes full of sadness.

"We've never tried to give one of the victims our blood before," he said. They'd never even had the chance to see if their blood would counteract a rogue's bite and keep the victim from changing into soulless evil. Emma was about to become their first experiment.

When Ace's wound closed, and the blood stopped, he moved aside. "Now, we wait."

"You guys go help the others, I'll stay here."

"You sure?" Kayla asked.

"Go."

Ace and Kayla left the room, and Decker set about cleaning Emma up. He wiped her face and neck. Her beautiful hair was matted with sticky blood, but there was nothing to be done about that now. To see her like this did something to him. Brought back memories he'd rather not recall and make him examine feelings he shouldn't have for her. He rinsed the sponge and started working on her arms, and that's when he spotted something. He turned her arm to get a better view of her inner wrist and sucked in a breath when he saw the mark.

He glanced at the door, then back at Emma. Did the mating mark now forming on her wrist belong to Ace? Or was there a possibility she was the mate of a rogue?

"Fuck," he whispered. One fate was worse than the other, but both caused him distress.

EMMA SWAM in a sea of darkness. The smell was sulfuric, and she could hardly breathe. She was drowning. Death was on her heels and there was no way to run fast enough. Just when she thought she would be pulled into an eternal black pit, a light so bright and warm filtered into her vision and she moved toward it. Finally, relief to her pain. As she continued to float further into the warmth of love, a female spoke to her.

"Emma, it's not your time."

"I don't want to go back."

A form took shape in front of her. She gasped at the beauty of the female. The angel's white wings a gorgeous contrast to her dark skin.

"A-are you real?" she whispered, afraid if she spoke too loudly the moment would shatter.

"I'm Eva, and yes, I am very much real." She smiled and moved closer.

"Then you're here to take me to my next life?"

Eva shook her head, causing her raven curls to bounce. "No. It's not your time."

"Then why am I here? I'm dead."

"You're not completely dead yet. They are trying to save you."

She cast her glance downward, expecting to see what? "I don't want to live in that world."

Eva laid a warm hand on her arm. "I know things are difficult. But you have a purpose yet unfulfilled in the world. You must help them survive. You must help him."

"Him?"

Eva's gentle touch moved down Emma's arm and to her wrist where she turned it over. "You have been chosen, Emma. Your mate needs you, you need him, and humanity needs you both."

She stared at the outline of a heart. The beginning of the mating mark. "Oh hell. Who is..."

Eva was gone, and the darkness swallowed her once again. Thoughts of the mark and the angel's words pounded in her head until she forced her eyes open.

"Well, glad to see you back here among the living." Decker sat in a chair next to her bed.

She went to push herself up, but he rushed forward. "Easy. You've had a bit of a hard time."

Emma tried to recall, and then everything came rushing back. Them in bed, the alarm and the attack. She felt her neck. Other than a little sore, there was no wound. She looked at her inner wrist and gasped out loud. So it was real.

"I'm not sure who that belongs to."

She stared at him. "What?"

"Ace gave you his blood. There's that, but the rogue bit you too."

"Are you saying I could be a rogue's mate?" That couldn't be right. "Am I going to turn into a rogue?" From what they knew, when bitten a person turned into the same soulless vampire that had bitten them. She wasn't even sure why she asked though. The angel said she had to help her mate so it was highly unlikely she could do that as a rogue. Her gut said not to worry.

"Shit! I'm going to become a vampire." The thought of drinking blood made her woozy.

"I'm only saying I have no idea, maybe Ace's blood negates the rogue bite," he snapped back.

"Why are you getting pissy with me? I'm the one with the problem here." Seriously, she was about to panic and he was the one acting like his life had just been altered.

"Sorry. Things have been bad around here."

She recalled the bloody floor. "Did we lose any?"

He scrubbed his face. "Three women, two men dead and one woman missing."

"Injured?" She tried to jump off the bed, but he stopped her.

"Under control, for now. You need to take a few minutes and finish healing."

She only nodded and lay back. "Does Ace have the mark?"

"I haven't talked to him since he left."

She looked at hers again. The black line forming the heart was now thicker. Darker. This couldn't be happening to her, and then a sudden realization came to her.

"Decker, is there a possibility it's your mark?"

He stared at her as if she had two heads. Talk about giving a girl a complex. She hurried to continue. "I mean, I gave you my blood and we almost..." Her face heated with how close they had come. How intimate they had been right before the alarm sounded.

"I don't have any marks."

Disappointment filled her. Why? She picked at her blanket and wanted nothing more than to rush from this room and find Ace. The need to know if fate was messing with her was unbearable. Decker must have sensed her turmoil.

"If you promise to stay here and behave, I'll go look for Ace. He's probably not far away."

"Thanks. I promise to behave. I really appreciate it."

He stood and without another word was gone. Now alone, the weight of everything that happened crashed down on her and she cried into her pillow. She was one person. How was she supposed to help humanity? She was already doing everything she knew how. Wasn't she? She had to wonder if there were other survivors out there that needed her. Her medical training might be limited, but she might be all they had left. The angel's words repeated in her head.

"You have been chosen, Emma. Your mate needs you, you need him, and humanity needs you both."

God, they were all screwed.

HE DIDN'T KNOW why he was so angry, but Decker wanted to

punch a wall. He chalked it up to an overabundance of adrenaline and fear. Fear that there might be a remote possibility Emma was his mate. It wasn't that he didn't have an attraction to her. That had been painfully obvious. He also felt a soul deep need to protect her. Keep her from harm's way, which apparently, he still sucked at. If not for his guilt that he was interested in another woman, he might have pursued Emma months ago. Even though he didn't bear a mark right now didn't mean shit. His friend Ryder had learned that and as far as they knew, there were no rules for this stuff.

He spotted Ace finishing up with another patient and headed in the vampire's direction.

"How's Emma?"

Decker glanced around. "We need to talk. Privately."

"Sure. I'm finished patching people up." He followed Decker to a vacant exam room.

"What the hell's going on?"

"Got a mating mark on you?" Might as well go straight to the point.

"What the fuck? Why would you ask that?"

"Cuz Emma now has one."

Ace's eyes widened, then he began checking his arms. "Son of a bitch." He held out his left wrist.

"Looks like the faint lines of a marking."

"But I never drank from Emma. Isn't that how this works? You have to drink from your mate?"

"You're barking up the wrong tree on that one, but if I heard the stories correctly, then yes. However, you know there are no fucking rules here. Every time we think we have this shit nailed down it changes." He stared at the faint lines of the infinity symbol on Ace's wrist. "Emma has a heart and it's much darker than yours. Whatever the hell that means."

"Shit, who knows." Ace scrubbed the stubble on his head. "I don't know what to do."

"Well, first thing is go talk to her. I made her promise to stay put while I found you and got answers."

"Yeah, I guess she's probably freaking out too." He moved for the door, then stopped. "Odd thing, I don't feel any weird urges." Ace rubbed the mark on his wrist. "Gordy was all crazy for his mate. Ryder too. Neither one could stay away from the women."

"Maybe it hasn't kicked in yet." Or, maybe the reason Decker was so pissed was because *he* was her mate.

Ace gave a curt nod then walked out, muttering under his breath. Once he was gone, Decker took a moment to collect his thoughts. Seeing the beginning of that mark on his brethren's wrist caused emotions he didn't like. If he analyzed it, he had almost slept with another man's mate, or had he? He looked at the ceiling. Had fate stepped in and stopped Emma and him from making a huge mistake? These days he questioned everything. Everything and nothing at all made sense.

CHAPTER NINE

EMMA TRIED to cling to her sanity and wiped her face on the blanket. She stared at the marking when the door opened. It was Ace, and she wasn't sure if she was happy to see him or not. The vampire towered in the doorway. His muscular frame taking up a lot of space. He was covered in blood, but knowing him it was doubtful any of it was his. She actually liked Ace. He called things like he saw them and took no shit from anyone. But there was his soft side. She'd seen him with baby Faith and it was a sight to see the big bad vampire hold such a tiny fragile bundle.

"Emma, may I come in?"

She didn't recall a time when Ace had seemed so timid as he was right now. This wasn't a good sign.

"Yes."

He stepped in and closed the door, then seemed to recall the state he was in and looked down at himself. "Sorry, I'm a mess."

"It's understandable. I heard we lost some people."

He nodded as he moved to sit in the chair in the tiny room. "So, Decker tells me you have a marking?"

She held out her wrist. "Looks like it." Part of her hoped Ace didn't have it, but that would mean she might be the mate of a rogue. The other half prayed he did carry it.

He swallowed, then held out his own wrist. While his mark was far lighter than hers, it was there.

"When?"

He shrugged. "It wasn't there this morning. At least not that I noticed. You?"

"Just showed up." She pulled her knees to her chest and wrapped her arms around her legs. "I..." How did she even begin to explain? "Did I die today?"

"You were close. That's why I gave you my blood, otherwise you would not have survived another hour."

"Thanks for saving me."

"Did I save you or did I condemn us both?"

She looked at him. "I saw the light everyone talks about."

He didn't speak, but looked at her, waiting for her to continue.

"There was a beautiful angel. Her name was Eva, and she told me I had to come back for him. That's when she showed me the mark." She tried to steady her breathing. "She was trying to tell me I had to come back to help my mate as well as humanity." She let out a nervous laugh. "Talk about a tall order."

He cast his gaze to the floor and Emma had never known Ace to look away from anything. "I'm sorry. You have to know I would never force this on you."

"I know that and neither would I. There's something else you should know. Decker and I... When the alarm sounded, we were in bed together." The thought of Decker sent her heart racing, and it made her gut roll. Here she was thinking of another man when they could never be together.

"I don't need to know about your past. Lord knows mine isn't clean."

"We were interrupted before anything happened, but I thought you should know."

He nodded. "Do you two have feelings for each other?"

"It was simply an itch we were both going to scratch." But was it? Why did it feel like so much more?

"Odd, I mean I like you Emma but I don't feel the soul-driving urges like the others did. I don't know what to make of this." He leaned forward in his chair and rested his elbows on his knees.

"I know what you mean, but seems in this new world someone else makes the rules. What do we do know?"

"Are you sure you don't have feelings for Decker? Be honest with both of us."

He was right. Now was not the time to try to hide. "Yes, but he doesn't have a mark. You and I do."

Ace thought for several moments before he stood. "Let me think on this. Are you feeling strong enough to come help us?"

All she'd wanted to do was leap from this bed and run out to assist. "Yes. I'm tired of being in here."

He held out his hand, and she slipped hers into his large palm. She waited for something, anything, but there was only warm skin. No electricity. No lustful desires. Nothing more than a friend helping her from bed. This wasn't a good sign, but maybe they just needed some time for things to settle. Time to know each other. As her feet hit the floor, she finally realized she was covered in blood. Pushing her hair aside, her fingers got stuck in a matted, sticky mess.

"I must look a horror," she said when Ace opened the door and they walked out.

"You look alive and no worse than the rest of us."

He was right. She had been close to death and even though their new world was a total mess, it was still good to be in it. She'd figure out the rest later once they had everyone patched up.

"HOW'S EMMA?" Kayla asked when she crossed Decker's path.

"Fine." He'd put more snarl into his words than he'd meant.

"Really? You two having problems?"

He stopped walking and looked at her. "Why would we have problems?" The grin on her face spoke of things he didn't like. What did she know?

"You two seemed to be hitting it off. Getting close. You know what I mean."

"I think you're reading things into this that aren't there." He wanted to say Emma had become marked but figured it wasn't his place to tell.

She looked as if she didn't believe a word he said but simply shrugged. "My mistake then. I won't keep you." She walked away, and he headed for his room for a quick shower.

Twenty minutes later, he was clean, dressed and in a state of fury and fear as he stormed to the compound's chapel. He'd been past it several times, but never inside. He pushed open the door and was relieved to find it empty. He headed straight for the altar and stood there staring at the stained-glass depiction of an angel holding white lilies. He had no idea if this would work, but he'd tried everything else.

"You rotten fuck." He curled his fingers into his palms. "Haven't you done enough damage? I don't need or want any more of your fated bullshit. Stop fucking with us, do you hear me?" By this time, he was shouting, and his voice echoed back at him. He briefly thought about walking into the sun, except that seemed to no longer have any effect on him. Now he understood why.

"I don't give a fuck what you throw at me. I'm not doing this again." It was then he sensed her and whirled around to face Emma.

"I'm sorry. I didn't mean to intrude, but I thought it would be empty in here." Emma shifted her weight, and he hated himself for making her uncomfortable.

"It doesn't matter. I was just leaving." He started to walk around her, but she stopped him.

"Can I help?"

"Not unless you can convince the bastard up there to stop fucking with my life."

Her eyes filled with sympathy as she tilted her head. "We're all upset about the deaths. The changes. It all sucks."

He shook his head. "No. You don't understand. I made a fucking deal and now he's going back on it."

Emma moved closer, reached out as if to touch him, then pulled back. "I'm sure a lot of us made promises to the Almighty if only he would fix this. Forgive us for our sins."

"I made no deal with that prick. He sought to end our existence without a thought. I was given a promise by a certain archangel." He shoved out his arm to show the faint marking on his right wrist. "I will never follow through on this. If I have to starve to death, become celibate, or burn this fucking mark from my skin so be it." He'd made a promise to his dying wife. He'd let her down once, he couldn't do it again.

She blinked as she stared at the faint lines that had started on his wrist. "They look just like the ones Ace has. What's going on?" This time she stared into his eyes, searching for answers he didn't have. Didn't want either because he was not traveling down that road. He couldn't.

"None of this makes sense, but it looks like fate might have given you two mates."

This time she stepped back. "That can't be right. I mean..." She rubbed her temple. "Am I supposed to choose between the two of you?"

"Don't worry, sweetheart, because I already stated my feelings on this matter. I'm not available. You and Ace will make a great couple." Then he moved past her. Unable to stand there for another second. Maybe once Ace and her made it official, his fucking mark would go away. If not, there was going to be hell to pay.

EMMA WAS FROZEN IN PLACE. It hurt to breathe and it was all she could manage to pull herself into a pew and sit down. She tried to force the panic that rose up like a violent beast into submission, but failed. It demanded possession of her body. Laughed at her plight. Her inability to breathe, the pains in her chest and the numbness that prickled her limbs. She gripped the pew in front of her and dug her fingers into the wood. The only sound that rang through the small church was the whooshing of her heartbeat in her ears.

It drowned out everything else.

Not now!

She'd not had a panic attack in months and even those had been slight. This... This bitch promised to take her to her knees. Vowed to blanket her in darkness.

Part of her wanted to cry for help because she was dying. The other, it said to shut the hell up because this was nothing more than an embarrassment. She would survive. She always did, but this time she had no medication to help her. She was all alone with her friend, misery.

Suck it up and remember how to breathe.

It had been awhile since she'd practiced the deep breathing technique that helped her get through her panic. Probably because there were too many other things to worry about. Simply surviving was a big one. Forcing herself to lean back, she straightened her spine, placed her right palm just under her breasts and began.

One deep breath in through the nose. A slow exhale out the mouth.

It wasn't working. She closed her eyes and tried to visualize the beach. It was her favorite place and always relaxed her. She'd never been able to go there enough and now may never see it again. She focused on the waves crashing to shore. The sun on her skin and the feel of sand between her toes then once again took a deep breath. This one was a bit easier and more steady as she exhaled. Emma knew from experience that this attack was going to take all she could muster to free herself from its clutches. Determination willed her to beat it. People were counting on her to help them. It's what she did. She healed others, and they had several injured that she needed to look after. The rest of this mess would have to wait until later. Maybe Ryder could call on his angel friends to help explain what was going on. There was no way Emma had two mates. She was not choosing based on some bullshit fate decided to throw at her. It wasn't fair to her or Ace and Decker. Not to mention that it seemed neither man wanted to be shackled to her forever.

The thought of Decker and the anger he carried worried her. What kind of deal had he made? She wanted to prod for more information, but didn't think he'd take it very well. Putting her mind elsewhere and onto other people's troubles managed to bring her back to reality. While her breathing still wasn't normal, it was close enough so she tested her legs. A little wobbly, but she'd manage. She had to leave the church. Being in it reminded her of things she wanted to forget. Like the fact she wouldn't be wearing a white dress and her father wouldn't be walking her down any aisle. Those fairytale days were in the past. It was time to adapt to the new world outside. One that required her to wear tactical vests and shoot at anything that threatened her or the others. She also had to come to grips with the possibility that like Kayla, Emma might end up a shifter. Or maybe even a vampire since she'd been given Ace's blood.

As she made her way to the door, she straightened. "If I'm to end up a shifter, then make me something bad-ass." She didn't want to end up being a mouse or some pitiful small creature. Being vulnerable was no longer in her plans.

CHAPTER TEN

IT HAD BEEN three weeks since Decker's outburst in the church with Emma and he'd managed to avoid her at all costs. There had been a near miss where he almost bumped into her and Ace as the two walked together to the mess hall for lunch one day. The sight of them together had caused his still faint mark to burn and his anger to rise, but he told both to kiss his ass and went about his duties. Now, the team was planning another trip to town to seek out Tatum before they headed out of the area for good. The weather held up and since they were into April, the chances of snow once out of the mountains was much slimmer. It was time. The wounded were healed enough to travel, and they had to try to find the others. Unity was their best bet for survival. Besides, he hoped that bastard Tegan might show up once they were on the road. He'd tried to call upon the archangel but was met with dead silence. Even Ryder had tried with the same results. They hadn't seen an angel all winter.

The fuckers had abandoned them completely.

He strapped on his vest and began checking his weapons when a familiar heat, followed by a soft voice, entered the room.

"I haven't seen you in forever," Emma said, strapping a blade to her thigh. Which, for some reason, he found sexy as hell.

"Been busy." He tried not to let his gaze linger too long. There was no reason to want her. She belonged to another man. Besides, he didn't need the shackle.

"I was thinking you might be avoiding me."

"Why would I do that? I'm not a fucking teenager."

She eyed him. "Because you have some unresolved issues." She moved her gaze to his wrist. "Still got the mark?"

He looked even though it had been there when he showered earlier and jerked himself off to thoughts of the damn female standing in front of him. "I tried to scrub it off, but no success. Maybe if you and Ace mated, mine will go away."

This time her lip curled. "Don't push it." She shoved a sidearm into her holster. "I'm of a mind to tell fate to fuck off."

He understood that, but what would happen to Emma if she chose to ignore her marking?

"Besides, Ace and I don't seem to have any attraction to each other. Nothing more than friends, anyway." She'd finished gearing up and was back to staring at him.

"What are you saying?" Since they were currently the only ones in the room, might as well shove this shit right out into the open.

"Nothing, other than Ace and I don't seem to be a match. Maybe it will come, but there is no mating for us anytime soon."

His mood turned more foul, if that was possible. What was he so pissed about? He tried to tell himself that Ace and Emma were fucking with him. He was convinced if they mated his mark would vanish, and he could go about his business. Not that he wasn't planning on just that, no matter what happened. He'd made a bargain with the archangel Tegan. Decker would fulfill his promise to help the survivors get established, then he could go. His days of misery on this fucked-up planet would be done and he could reunite with his wife and daughter. He would finally be at peace. He wasn't letting Tegan out of *that* agreement. Not a chance in this Hell or the next.

He looked at Emma, there was something different about her but he wasn't able to name it. "You been feeling okay?"

She offered a surprised look. "I'm surprised you care. Actually, I've never felt better."

He shouldn't but he did. Cared way more than was appropriate for a man who was supposed to be grieving his dead wife. "Well, good to hear. That still doesn't mean you can go on this expedition."

She only grinned. "I don't need your permission. I'm part of Ace's team. At least he understands that I need to do this."

Suddenly, he wanted to kill the other vampire, and his opportunity just walked in the room. His stride toward Ace couldn't get him there fast enough.

"What the hell are you doing?"

Ace offered a stunned glance, then grabbed a knife. "Let me guess, you're referring to Emma going out tonight?"

"You know I am."

"Seems to me that's her choice. Why are your panties in a wad over it?" Ace cocked a brow and waited.

"Because she's our medical personnel."

Right then, Ryder stepped in. "You two need to stop this shit. Either beat the fuck out of each other and get it over with or Decker just fucking admit your defeat."

He stared at his long-time friend. "Defeat?"

Ryder sighed. "It's obvious to everyone but you that you care about Emma. Just fucking admit it. We all know that you're her mate. You've been walking around here for weeks like you're ready to kill anyone who crosses your path."

Decker tried not to take a step back at those words. "Of course, I care. I care about every soul here."

"Definite denial," Kayla said from behind Ryder.

Decker walked back and grabbed a radio. "Fine. Do whatever you want. At least I stated the obvious and can have a clear mind knowing that." He headed for the door. "I'm going to meet Carlos and go over our plans." Then he left, not sure who he was more pissed at.

EMMA TOLD herself she didn't care about Decker and how he felt, but in reality, she did. She and Ace had several conversations over the past few weeks as he helped her tend to the injured. They had both come to the conclusion that there was no way they were fated, destined—or whatever the hell you wanted to call it—to be together. They felt nothing more than friendship for each other. The two even had dinner in his quarters one evening to discuss the future and see where things led. They went down a path of a few kisses that were more like kissing a sibling than a lover and both had decided they would no longer pursue a relationship. Decker had even entered their conversation, and it was then Ace had told her Decker had lost his pregnant wife to the Red Death. Everything made more sense after that. Emma admitted the way her body responded to the pain-in-the-ass vampire and Ace hadn't felt one ounce of jealous rage over it. It was only more proof that Ace and Emma were not fated mates. She was certain Decker was the one who needed her and Ace agreed so he formed a plan to prove it.

She got Ace off to the side. "I'm not fond of this deception," she whispered.

"We discussed this. You wanted to go on the mission, and I'm willing to have you on my team. I can't help it if that fact is going to drive Decker crazy." He finished strapping his vest on. "At some point he's going to come to his senses."

"He's insufferable." She glared at Ace, probably a little too hard because he laughed.

"Of course, he is." He handed her a flashlight. "He's too stubborn to admit what's staring him in the face. Not to mention that men hate being wrong. It's just how we are."

"Thanks for being a friend."

"Anytime you need me, I'm here for you."

Emma was grateful for Ace. He was a good friend and also proved to be an excellent assistant in the infirmary. But, seeing

Decker, being close to him was difficult. Her body wanted him and her mind wanted to heal the wound he carried around. Easier said than done. She was half tempted to stay here at the compound and let the rest of the team go. However, she needed to get outside and hoped fresh air and a good sprint might help cool off her libido. Besides, she still needed to check out the hospital for any supplies since they were planning to leave in a few days. They had a lot of work to do and needed all the hands they could get. This time, the team going was bigger and consisted of several of the human men. They were still using the darkness though since the vampires had issues with the sun.

"Let's head out," Ryder said and everyone gathered in the corridor. The plan was for the vampires to go out on foot while Kayla opened a portal for the rest of the team. Vampires were able to travel at a much faster speed than humans and would probably get there shortly after the rest of them. The only immortals going through the portal would be Kayla, Ryder, and Ace. They didn't want to send the rest of their team into danger without some bad-ass backup.

The vampires left via the front door and Emma knew that Ryder was in contact with his men, as well as Decker, using the special link they had that allowed them to communicate using telepathy. They gave them a twenty-minute head start before Kayla opened the portal and everyone began to go through.

Seconds later, they were back in the middle of Gettysburg. Emma remained alert for any signs of danger, but the darkness was always a barrier. She often wondered why they never found any of those fancy night vision goggles at the compound. Giving herself a moment to adjust, she suddenly realized she was able to make out every person around her. Kayla's strawberry blonde hair, with the pink streaks that framed the woman's face, were as clear as if the sun was shining on her friend. She turned her focus to Ryder. The tribal tattoos that ran along the left side of his neck took on an energy of their own. They pulsed with life.

She quickly looked away right as Ace came up next to her and she dared not make eye contact with him.

"Ready to check the hospital again?"

"Yes. No." A sensation she wasn't able to explain crawled over her skin.

"What's wrong?" This time it was Kayla who spoke.

"I... I can't explain it, but I sense something." She didn't even want to touch the fact she was seeing better in the dark than ever before. Something was happening to her.

The others looked around, then Decker stepped into the crowd and that's when Ace shook his head. Emma knew what he was thinking. He thought it was Decker she sensed, but deep down she knew that wasn't it. There was something else.

"No, Ace, you're wrong. There's something else out there."

"Explain it best you can, Emma," Decker said and god his voice felt like silk wrapped around her skin.

She tried not to shiver, but focused in the distance to the south of them. In the direction of their compound. "I feel some kind of energy. I think." How was she even sure with him now standing so close and throwing her off balance? "There's a slight glow of light in the distance." This time she pointed. Decker followed, and she noticed he actually squinted.

"I don't see anything." He looked around. "Anyone else?"

The rest of the team muttered a no and Decker looked at her like she was insane. Maybe she was, but her gut said something was out there and it needed to be investigated.

"Well, I see something so I propose we check it on the way back to the compound."

"That would mean you'd have to walk back. That will take too long and risk my men," Ryder replied.

"I'll take her," Decker spoke up. "Carlos can check out the hospital again. Emma and I will look for Tatum, then start heading back and find out what Emma's sensing."

"It's your call then. For now, let's get moving as we're running out of darkness." Ryder moved his team west to scout for any usable vehicles or fuel.

"Ace, you're in charge of this unit, do you have any objections?"

"Whatever you want, Decker."

Emma was certain there was a slight chuckle in Ace's reply. The vampire likely believed Decker was proving everyone's theory that he was actually her mate. She, on the other hand, wasn't sure what she thought about this entire mess. One thing was certain, everything in her gut told her they needed to check out whatever was out there in the distance.

Decker lifted his head and took a deep breath.

"Did you just sniff the air," she asked.

"I'm trying to find the girl's trail."

She shook her head. This man was full of endless surprises.

HER SCENT WAS PLAYING havoc with his head. Why had he decided it was a good idea to take Emma on some damn goose chase? He needed his head examined. Or cut off.

"I think we should head this way." He didn't wait to see if she followed, his entire body reacted to her presence and knew she was behind him. He hated himself. Despised this new world and part of him was even angry with Emma for putting him in this position. It was difficult to rationalize this wasn't her fault.

"So, why are you lying about what's going on with you?"

"What? I don't understand what you mean." She moved next to him and fought to keep up with his stride. He should slow down, but he was too angry right now.

"Don't play with me, Emma. I can sense when you're lying. Back there, something else was going on with you."

"Wait, you can sense when I'm lying?" Her voice was filled with anger and he didn't give a shit.

"I can sense many things about people. Seems this fucking mark you gave me, just amplifies your feelings."

Her brows dipped. "I gave you? Excuse me, but I don't know why you think I gave you this mark and not the other way around." She stopped walking. "Ace has the same marking or did you forget that?"

Like he needed a reminder of that. "I know full fucking well what Ace has and why haven't you two mated?" He'd hoped if the two did, his mark would go away and he could continue on with his plan. The promise he'd made to his dying wife.

"Did you hit your head when I wasn't looking? Because I thought I already went over this." She started walking at a much brisker pace. Her foul mood filled the air and coated his tongue. Why did he find it sexy? He really was fucked in the head.

"You're not trying hard enough."

She turned on him. "You didn't just say that?"

"I believe I spoke clearly, but if you'd like me to repeat it in another language, I can. Perhaps Spanish? You do speak your father's native tongue, don't you?"

Her mouth dropped. "How do you know anything about my father?"

"I thought it was common knowledge?"

"I've only told a few people about my family."

He shrugged. "I guess I heard it somewhere then." Actually, he just knew it. Like he knew many things about her and that just fueled his anger further.

"No, I don't need you to repeat it. I understand perfectly that you're an *el cabrón*."

Why did he want to kiss that smug look off her face? "Yes, I'm an asshole, dickhead, bastard, everything you want to call me." He stepped into her space. "Sugar, when you've lived my life it becomes necessary to harden yourself until everything rolls off. It's called survival."

She slammed her hands to her hips. "One can still allow things to *roll* off and not be an asshole." She tilted her head to look up at him.

"I wonder if there's anything left inside of you, or are you cold and empty in here?" She jabbed a finger into his chest.

This woman had no idea just how empty he was. How unbearably cold he felt every second of his miserable existence except when she was near. He was a predator now. Decker didn't deserve peace and somewhere along the way, he'd finally realized that this was his punishment. The deal he'd made with the archangel Tegan. The one that promised if Decker fulfilled his mission, then he could finally leave this world and be with his wife and daughter. No, his punishment was to forever exist without the two he had loved most. Those were terms he wasn't sure he could ever come to live with. He didn't like failure. Hated it when a mission didn't go as planned, but when he failed his wife and daughter... How did one ever come back from that? He didn't deserve to. Everything in him died that day. Yet, here he stood with this fiery female in front of him and he felt anything but dead.

He had to protect her from the world and himself. He hated being near her and the feelings she stirred up, yet he couldn't stand to be away. He was so screwed.

CHAPTER ELEVEN

EMMA FELT the first wave of cold and it wasn't until the second that she realized what she was experiencing came from Decker. Her words had opened something inside of him. Something dark and empty. All she wanted to do in this moment was offer him comfort, warmth and kindness. The world around them stopped, and she realized that fate had brought them together for a reason. He needed her. The guardian angel's words came back to her, and she was more convinced than ever that *this* was the man she was supposed to help. Decker needed a lifeline back to the real world and she would make sure he got it.

She flattened her hand on his chest, and even through his tactical vest, his heat seeped into her. There was no coldness inside him. Not to her, anyway. He brought his own hand to hers as if to move her away and the second they touched she saw it. A soft white energy swirled between their fingers. Emma was positive she was the only one to notice and wondered where it had come from. Rather than question it, she raised up on her toes and kissed him before he could back away.

At first, his body went rigid, but she pressed on. Laying her other palm on his chest, she kept her lips against his. His mouth parted slightly, and she took full advantage by sweeping her tongue inside. He tasted like mint, and she was surprised, though she wasn't sure why. It only took her delving a little deeper before his hands gripped her hips and jerked her so close, she was able to feel his erection against her. He returned her kiss, and it was full of hunger and desperation and she wished they were anywhere but here right now.

They both fell into the spell of the moment. Their bodies close yet not close enough, and the energy she'd witnessed crackle between their fingers now circled them. It was both beautiful and frightening, but before she could break the kiss and ask him about it, an explosion rocked the darkness. Decker ripped away from her and shoved her behind him as he faced down whatever had disrupted the night.

"What is it?" She knew that as she asked, Decker was contacting his people along with Ryder. Everyone he had a mental link with, to inquire if they knew what happened as well as making sure they were all safe.

"Carlos says the hospital was blown up."

When she gasped, he quickly continued.

"No one was hurt, but the fucking rogues are there," he growled and his body went tense. "We need to make our way back to them."

"Of course." She heard him mutter under his breath how she shouldn't be here. Emma did have to admit, she was nervous after her last near-death encounter with a rogue. It wasn't going to stop her from stepping up to help though. What else could she do? Opening a portal back to the compound while in the middle of a fight was too risky. The rogues might follow them and put the entire compound in danger. She only hoped that the bastards weren't already there and causing havoc again.

"Why do you suppose we went months without attacks and suddenly they won't leave us alone?" She slipped into a trot next to Decker as he led them back toward the others. When they crossed the street, he stopped behind a broken-down gas station.

"Why are we stopping?" she whispered.

"We have company."

She looked around and finally saw the outline of two figures. One petite while the other towered over the smaller one. Instantly, she knew who they were.

"Tatum and that demon." The two were heading in their direction and it didn't take long for them to arrive.

"I should have known you were the reason the rogues showed up," Tatum hissed.

"Nice to see you too." Decker's reply held just as much bite, making Emma wonder what happened between these two when he'd spent the day in town.

"Why are you here?" the girl asked, arms folded over her skinny frame.

This time Emma laid a hand on Decker's arm and stepped beside him. After the last time, she dared not move between him and the girl or the demon. "Hi, Tatum. Remember me?"

Decker let out a growl, and she just squeezed his arm rather than tell him to zip it. The man may not want to admit they belonged together, but he was certainly acting like they did.

"Yeah, I remember you. You the leech's food source?"

"No, just a friend. Tatum, we are here to gather supplies and any survivors. We plan to leave in a few days and meet up with other survivors."

"Good for you, but you won't find much left."

"Will you come with us?" Emma asked then placed her focus on the demon. There was something about the creature that intrigued her. It took her a moment, but finally she placed it. There was some kind of energy source coming from the demon, and it called to her. She'd not even realized she was moving closer until Decker grabbed her arm.

"What the hell are you doing?"

Emma shook off her trance-like state. "There's something about the demon. Something... familiar."

DECKER'S HEART raced when Emma started moving closer to the demon. It was like she was under some kind of spell and he didn't like it. Not one damn bit. "We don't have time, the others need us."

Emma seemed to regain her senses and nodded. "Of course. Let's go."

They moved down the street, keeping close to the buildings. Decker noticed the demon followed them and Tatum came in at the rear. He wasn't sure he trusted that beast, and especially not around Emma. It seemed to have some kind of effect on her. He was going to have to keep an eye not only on Emma, but the demon as well as their enemies. Not a great situation to be in, therefore, he reached out to Carlos.

I've got my hands full. Watch this demon that's tailing us but don't harm it unless it makes a move against one of us.

Got it, sire.

At least now he could breathe slightly better. He stopped and looked over his shoulder at Emma. "Weapons ready?"

"Yes," she whispered.

Then he glanced at Tatum. "Is Hugh going to fight on our side?" Before the girl could answer, Emma spoke up.

"He will."

He only looked at her. Something strange was going down with this female, but he didn't have time to figure it out or ask questions. Another explosion rocked the ground under their feet.

"I'm about as sick of these fucking rogues as I can get," he growled then slipped around the corner of the building where he met up with Carlos, Ryder and Ace.

"Where's Kayla?" Decker asked, knowing full well that Ryder hated having his mate out of his sight.

"She's taken a couple of men and gone back to the compound for some heavy weapons."

"They blew up the hospital," Ace said. "They know what we're here for, fucking bastards."

"Did you guys find anything worth grabbing?"

"Yep." Ryder grinned right when the sound of engines roared to life and three moving trucks rounded the corner. As they screeched to a halt, he noticed Axel and Jaden in the back of one of the trucks, each with a flame thrower.

Adrenaline pumped through his veins. "Let's toast these fuckers."

Everyone moved out, heading in the direction of the last known location of the rogues, except for two men left to guard the trucks. Apparently, Ryder's team had come across a moving truck rental lot. It was like striking gold, which they really needed right now.

They hadn't made it a block when the rogues appeared out of thin air and with them, several demons. Fucking hell, Decker wondered how many rogues there were now. The damn things seemed to reproduce like rabbits wanting world domination. For a moment, he contemplated if they would ever win this war against Lucifer and his minions. The only chance any of them stood was if Lucifer's son, Logan, was able to locate his father and finally end the demon king's reign.

Someone fired a flame thrower into the thick of at least half a dozen rogues and demons, charring them almost instantly. He was glad to see this weapon, it would come in handy to take out the enemy en mass. Decker charged a demon heading in their direction and fired a bullet between its eyes. It was enough to take it down while someone else came along and made sure it was dead by either burning or beheading it. He tried to keep an eye on Emma while he took out more rogues and cursed her for being here, but so far, she was holding her own. There was a small part of him that was rather proud of that fact. He might never want to be involved in a serious relationship again, but that didn't mean he didn't care for her.

More fire blasted past him and heated the air as the screams of death and a stench so foul filled his lungs it caused him to gag. He took out two more rogues, but they came as fast as they were taken down. Every time he slayed one, he wondered if that one had been a survivor of the Red Death. They knew a rogue vampire's bite could change a human into one of them, but demons also created rogues so they never knew who they were really killing. Not that it mattered because in the end, any human turned was already gone.

From the corner of his eye, he watched Emma to make sure she was safe. For some reason, she stuck close to Tatum's pet demon, which seemed to be protecting both women. He was good with that as long as the demon didn't turn on Emma. He'd have to rain Hell down on the beast if that happened.

"More incoming!" Hunter shouted as he fired off several rounds.

Not much caused Decker to worry, but the sight of so many rogues bearing down on them that he couldn't even count them all caused his heart to skip a few beats. Where the hell had they come from? Both Axel and Jaden blasted the rogues with the fire launchers, but the bastards continued to surround them. The demon, Hugh, fought off several as they tried to reach Tatum and Emma. Decker's panic rose to proportions he disliked immensely when Emma had to fire her weapon and take down a rogue. She was a nurse, not a killer, and he had to get to her.

Protect her, his internal voice screamed. He couldn't let another woman die on his watch, yet several rogues filled the space between him and Emma.

"We might be fucked," Ryder shouted as he shoved his blade into the neck of a demon.

CHAPTER TWELVE

EMMA TRIED NOT to panic as they were quickly surrounded. She had no idea how or why there were so many rogues, but all she could do was fire her weapon and pray.

Use your power to save them.

"What?" She swore the words had streamed into her mind, but that couldn't be right. She didn't have any telepathic abilities.

Use your power to save them.

This time she swung to look at Hugh, who she somehow knew had spoken to her. "I don't have any power." Even the words didn't feel correct as she stared at the white energy that was being emitted from the demon. He was filled with some kind of power so why didn't he use it on these rogues?

"You are a witch. You can save them." This time Hugh spoke in a gravel-filled voice.

Emma blinked, unsure she heard correctly. If not for the fact they were in deep shit, she would have laughed. Yet, part of her was intrigued by the demon's words and wondered if the changes she was experiencing had anything to do with what he was trying to communicate.

"Use me, I am meant to help you." Hugh reached out with his claw-tipped hand, and Emma was drawn to him. Everything around her faded into the background. Even Decker's shouts of her name faded into the distance as she stretched out her hand and touched the demon.

The second they connected electricity sparked. The world righted, and a current of power ripped through her body and nearly sent her stumbling backward. She saw everything with new eyes. Lines of blue light lit up the sky in a vibrant pattern of criss-cross lines that went far into the horizon.

Use the magic Gaia offers and save your friends. Hugh went back to speaking in her mind. *I am your conduit.*

Emma went on instinct. Letting go of Hugh, the energy still pulsed through her, around her and she knew she had to harness it. Lifting her arms to the sky, she let the words spill from her mouth.

"Gaia, Earth Goddess, hear my call and free us from the confines of this space. Save us from this evil that would cause us harm."

The ground rumbled and the blue lights hummed in electric power before the sky went black. Silence blanketed Emma as she tried to pull her thoughts together.

"What the hell just happened?"

It was the sweet sound of Decker's surprised voice.

"I'd say we were somehow transported. Kayla?" Ryder said.

"Not me," Kayla replied.

"I think it was me." Emma finally found her voice. "Is everyone here?" She held her breath for an eternity while she waited for a reply.

"I think so," Decker replied. "Where are we and what do you mean it was you?"

Emma looked around and thought they were in the location she had spotted earlier. The one that held the energy she'd seen, but as she moved closer, she realized it held the same color blue as the lines she'd seen. She searched for Hugh and finally spotted him near Tatum.

"Hugh."

The demon looked her way.

"What is this place?"

"A gate."

"Shit, he talks," Ryder said.

Kayla moved closer and Ryder tried to pull her to him, but she smacked his arm away. "Stop being so over protective." She stepped in front of Hugh. "You're different from the others."

He dipped his horse-shaped head and folded his wings into his body. The same blue light Emma had seen earlier swirled around him. Consumed him and then transformed him.

"Shit." Tatum backed away.

Hugh, the demon, was now a six and a half-foot tall man dressed in modern day attire of jeans and a long-sleeve tee. His dark hair was pulled back at the nape of his neck and the only thing that looked out of place was his eyes. They were the same brilliant blue as the lines across the sky.

He dipped his head. "Forgive me, it is much easier to speak your language while in your form. My real name is difficult for your tongue so you may call me Jag."

"Jag. What are you exactly?" This time Emma asked the question.

"I am a Grotog demon, a creation of Gaia the Mother Goddess of the Earth." He focused his brilliant gaze on Emma. "And you are a daughter of my ancestors. You carry Gaia's magic inside you. You are a witch and I, your conduit to her magic."

"Umm." Emma blinked and was at a total loss for words yet had so many questions.

"Let's start with where the hell are we?" Decker stepped next to her all tall, powerful and protective. She might even swear his chest was puffed out.

"This is a gate. There are many in the world. Unlike a portal the shifter opens to where she wishes to go, a gate only goes between two places."

"What's the point of that?" Kayla asked. "A portal sounds like a much better option."

"True, but there are limitations. You can only go where you've been or a location you've seen on a map. Portals also have a limited range. A gate is true every time and once you learn to read them, you know exactly where you're going. You can travel across the world in seconds." He waved his hand toward the blue light. "And only a witch or one of my species can see them."

"Emma, you see this gate?" Decker asked.

"Yes. It's the source I saw earlier." She moved closer to it. "Where does this go?"

Jag moved closer. "See the markings here?" He pointed and Emma noticed, to the right of the swirling energy mass, some symbols.

"I see them."

"Those will tell you the location this gate leads to. This one is to a place you call Kentucky."

Emma reached out and touched the symbols. Her fingers moving across electrified air, and a picture entered into her head. "I see..." She closed her eyes and tried to focus. "I see grass that's nearly green, and a street lined with houses." Her heart pounded with excitement as she looked at Jag. "How do I use this thing?"

"You simply walk through it and you're there. It operates much like a portal in that sense, but the gate is always there and there are thousands. You just need to know where to find them."

She started to move when a strong hand grabbed her arm.

"Oh no you don't," Decker said. "It's almost daylight and we need to get back. We can talk more about these gates and form a plan to check this out further."

She knew he was right, but what was on the other side called to her. It felt warmer than where they were. "You're right, but I think Tatum and Jag need to come back with us." She turned back to the demon, who now looked nothing like one. "Jag?"

"I am your servant for as long as either of us lives." He gave a deep bow. "I can take us all back to your compound so the shifter doesn't need to expend her energy with a portal."

"I'm not sure I like this plan," Decker stated.

"I trust him," she replied.

Tatum shifted. "Umm, I don't know that I trust you guys."

"Well, seems we are all on the same page with our trust issues. So, let's just go for it. My gut tells me it's a good thing," Ryder spoke up and the next thing they knew, magic crackled and once again the scenery changed.

⌒○○○○○⌒

DECKER MUTTERED obscenities under his breath as his boots hit the concrete floor of the compound. That demon had too easily moved the entire group to their location. Though, he had told Tatum where they were hiding out, so she likely told the demon at some point. He'd be keeping both eyes on that demon, and he had a lot of questions.

"Jag, if you don't mind, Ryder and I would like to ask you some questions."

"I'm coming with," Emma said. Determination lighting her brown eyes.

"Don't you have wounded to attend to?"

She looked around at the team. "Anyone need me?"

A round of no's sounded, and Kayla touched her arm. "He's stalling to keep you away."

Emma tore at her vest, removing it. "Obviously, but this involves me and I'm coming." Her chin tilted upward. "Lead the way."

"Stubborn woman." Decker spun on his boot and headed down the corridor, expecting them to follow. He heard Kayla telling Tatum about the showers as she led the girl away. He was glad for that. At least he wouldn't have to deal with the snotty teen.

He shoved open the door to a large conference room where a big oak table took up center stage and was surrounded by several leather chairs. While he was too edgy to sit, he moved to the chair to the right and let Ryder take the head. This was the other vampire's place after all, and even though he was twitchy, he pulled out his chair and sat. He did, however, lay his pistol on the table, keeping his hand on it.

"Seriously?" Emma raised a brow. "You that nervous?"

"One can never be too careful," he commented.

Jag sat across from Decker. "He has good reason to be cautious. Many demons are pure evil."

"Yeah, like the ones who helped create the fucking rogues," Decker added. "And let's not forget Morbus, who we have to thank for this plague."

"Morbus isn't evil, he's cursed to forever bring destruction until he meets his fate."

"Would that be a blade through his neck?' Ryder asked.

Jag leaned forward. "I suppose that's one fate, but his curse ends when he meets his destined mate which is rather difficult to find when you're locked away."

"Sounds to me like you're defending him," Decker point out.

"That's because I am. Lucifer used Morbus to spread rot throughout the world. He placed the curse on the demon, then locked him away so he could keep Morbus from breaking it. I, for one, hope he's never found."

"That's a rotten thing to do to someone." Emma's eyes held a great deal of sympathy. It didn't surprise Decker. After all, she had the kindest heart of probably anyone in the compound. It was she who had saved baby Faith. She still looked after the child even though everyone had taken to the baby girl. Faith was the only light in their future, but Decker often found it difficult to hold the child. She brought memories of everything he'd lost.

"Well, as we all know, Lucifer is rotten to the core," Ryder said.

"Morbus will be difficult to contain. He's learned from past experience how to avoid capture," Jag pointed out, only confirming what Decker was already concerned about.

"While I can sympathize with the demon, it means we are

screwed as long as he's running amok." Ryder scooted his chair back for Kayla, who'd just walked in to plop in his lap.

Decker looked at his friend with a bit of envy. Even though fate had stepped in and decided Ryder and Kayla belonged together, it was clear to see they loved each other. He would admit, fate made a wise choice with these two. He then looked at Emma and wondered why fate was pushing them together. Part of him wanted her. The part that was all male and needed to feel a warm female beneath him. The other half hated himself for what he wanted. It wasn't supposed to be like this. He'd made a deal with Tegan when the archangel had asked Decker, Ryder, Shade and Wolfe to step up and care for survivors. In exchange, the archangel had shared his blood to make certain the vampire primordials were inoculated against the Red Death. Decker had also made Tegan vow that once humanity was established, Decker could be released from his promise. Tegan would make sure that Decker died and would then reunite with his wife and daughter in the next world.

His gut said that was never going to happen. He looked at the symbol that had darkened on his wrist. It was the infinity, a symbol that he had become immortal and only taking his head would end him now. When he looked back up, Emma was staring back at him. She deserved better than him. Hell, Ace was a far better match for her. The other vampire didn't carry Decker's baggage.

"So, is the mating mark I carry the reason these witchy abilities have suddenly showed up?" She shifted in her chair. "I noticed tonight when we went out that things had changed. My vision was better, obviously I saw the energy for that gate, but I also feel different."

Jag looked surprised. "May I see your mating mark?"

Emma nodded and extended her arm, exposing her wrist. When the demon touched the marking, Decker nearly came unglued. Out of the corner of his eye, he caught Ryder grinning. No doubt his so-called friend found this entire situation hysterical. Decker really needed to pull his shit together.

"This mark has not been seen in many years, but it is a mark some carry. It's often brought on when a female comes in close contact with her mate."

Well, now they were getting somewhere. Looked like this demon might hold some of the answers they were looking for. "So, why then did Ace and I get the marking the same time as Emma?" Decker settled back in his chair waiting for a response.

Jag lifted a shoulder. "You both came into contact with your mate."

"But we don't have another female here that has the mark," Kayla piped up.

"It is possible Ace's mate is not here. Perhaps they had contact prior and the mark now shows itself. Or, she simply hasn't gotten her mark yet."

"Wait. So how do you know that I'm not Ace's mate? I mean he gave me his blood to save my life, and that's when the mark showed up." Emma fidgeted in her seat.

"Because you and the vampire across the table have the same energy source. The marks don't always show instantly. They can take time to develop on either mate."

"Whoah, so you can see their energy?" Kayla's eyes widened.

"Of course. Just as I see that you and your mate have the same energy. Mates are a match made by a higher power and it is never wrong."

"Never?" Decker asked.

Jag shook his head. "Never."

Well, fuck his life.

CHAPTER THIRTEEN

EMMA DIDN'T SLEEP at all, but despite that she felt energized. She'd sat most of the morning talking to Jag, still amazed at his transformation into a human. Though not half as amazed as learning more about her ancestors. While Jag couldn't tell her how far back the demon gene entered her family pool, he thought it was a few hundred years. Both she and Jag were able to perform magic on their own, but together she was much more powerful. He'd taught her some small parlor tricks like levitating objects and she was surprised at the ease in which she was able to do it. There was so much for her to learn, yet everything seemed to come naturally. It was as if she'd been doing magic her entire life. Granted, she wouldn't be doing anything big for a while and needed Jag to guide her, but he had indicated in time she might be able to heal the injured with magic. That excited her.

For now, she was dressing to head back out to the gate. Decker and Ryder had agreed to take her and Jag back and check out what was on the other side. After pulling her unruly curls into a ponytail, she grabbed a jacket and headed out the door. She wondered how Decker was faring after the news that the two of them were definitely chosen to be together. He had some demons in his closet that he'd yet to talk to her about. She wondered if he ever would, but one thing was for certain, they needed to talk about their current situation. She didn't want to push him, just get him to open up a little.

As she headed out her door, she nearly ran into Decker.

"Oh were you waiting for me?"

"I don't like this. I just have a bad feeling deep in my bones." He started down the corridor, and she had to increase her pace to keep up with him.

"Do you think it's something with the gate?" Her excitement turned to a jitter of nerves. They didn't know what they'd find on the other side.

"I'm not sure. Just be cautious is all I'm saying." He glanced over at her.

She grinned. "Careful there, Decker, I might get the wrong idea and think you care."

As they rounded the corner, Decker replied, "Don't read anything into this, Torres."

The use of her last name was his way of putting distance between them. Fine, she'd give him all the damn space he wanted. Moments later, they met up with Jag and Ryder. Kayla came running down the hall to join them. She and Ryder were hardly ever separated. If Emma could figure this gate thing out, between her, Kayla and Jag, they should be able to go just about anywhere. Maybe they could find more survivors. Kayla had gotten Tatum to open up and admit there had been other survivors, but they had moved on. To where, the girl didn't know and wouldn't say why she hadn't gone with them.

"Are we ready?" Jag asked.

"Let's roll out," Ryder replied as he took his mate's hand.

Seconds later, they all stepped out of the portal and stood in front of the gate. Even with the overcast skies, the sun was still bright and Emma found herself checking on Decker. No smoke and his skin appeared fine. He'd finally confessed a few days ago that he no longer had an issue with the sun like the other vampires. She was grateful for that, but it seemed like another sign he was ignoring.

"This gate leads to a place in Kentucky," Jag confirmed again after looking at the symbols Emma had studied last night.

"Emma, use your power to open it," Jag said.

"How do I do that?"

"Hold your hand near the symbols and feel the power. Think about the gate opening and it shall obey your command."

Sounded simple enough, but she was a bit skeptical. "Okay." Emma stood next to Jag and held her hand near the symbols. She stared at the blue lights and sent a mental command. A buzz started in her ears, then warmth caressed her skin as a gentle breeze lifted her hair. The colored energy she'd seen before turned from blue to a vibrant green and the gate itself turned into a circular mass of blue light filled with white.

"Well done. The gate is open and ready."

"I'll take the lead," Decker said and without hesitation, he stepped into the mass of lighted energy then was gone.

"I'll go next," she offered, knowing that Ryder would take up the rear. Before anyone could reply, Emma stepped into the energy and a micro-second later out the other side. It was more like stepping through a doorway, which was unlike a portal that took a few seconds and you felt the pull on your body. She liked this much better.

Jag, then Kayla followed by Ryder, came up behind her as she looked around at the scene in front of her. They stood in the middle of a street. A few cars lined each side of the quiet neighborhood where large houses stood with their once manicured lawns now full of weeds and overgrowth. Out of the eerie quiet a pair of boots slapped the asphalt carrying an angry Decker who stormed right up to Jag.

He grabbed the demon by the shirt and jerked him closer. "What kind of fucking game are you playing?" he snarled.

"Decker!"

HE BARELY HEARD Emma cry his name as he stared at the demon through a red haze. "Fucking answer me."

"You do realize this demon can wipe up the street with you, *Vampire*."

That voice made his haze grow even darker as he dropped Jag and whirled to focus his rage on the one who deserved it most. "You rotten fuck."

The archangel, Tegan, simply raised a brow and snapped his golden wings flat to his back where they were absorbed into his body and vanished. Even the wind stopped and the very air surrounding them arched with a power so intense it nearly hurt to breathe. "And I can destroy you without blinking."

Decker moved into the archangel's personal space. "You were behind this." He rolled his fingers into a fist, ready to punch the smug son of a bitch in the face. When he wound back, he found himself unable to follow through and Emma was at his side.

"Decker! You can't hit an angel!"

"I could if the bastard would release me." Decker might even consider ripping his throat out. "Let go of me. We have unfinished business."

"We do?" Tegan crossed his arms over his chest and pinned his intense green eyes on Decker.

"You promised me if I helped you, I could eventually leave."

The angel's gaze softened. "I did, but you don't belong in their world. That promise was my mistake."

Decker was granted movement again and lowered his arm. He wasn't sure why he didn't follow through with punching Tegan, but the angel leaned closer and whispered, "You must face your demons before you can move on. This world needs you."

Ryder stood on Decker's other side. "Is this why you decided to show up? To give Decker a lecture?"

"No, but he is needed here. You all are needed."

"Why me? Why is it so important for myself... For Ryder or any of the other primordials to be here?"

"Because we lost too much the last time humanity died out."

"What?" Kayla moved closer. "What do you mean?"

Just then the air stirred and a beautiful woman holding a baby stepped out of nowhere. Her snow-white wings dusted with silver was a clear indicator of who she was. The pure angel that was now Tegan's mate and the infant their newborn son. Rhea smiled. "Humanity prospered thousands of years ago."

"Yes, we know that," Decker said with little patience.

"No. Civilized humans became extinct before evolution started again. There is a reason many archeologists are starting to consider this philosophy as they uncover ancient ruins that they cannot explain. Humans were here long before you believe, and they did excel with the help of more advanced beings." Rhea rocked the small bundle in her arms. "But Morbus spread sickness and wiped everyone out."

"Everyone?" Emma whispered.

The angel met her gaze. "No mortal was left alive. Humanity had to be started again, and that is the evolution you know today. Along the way, angels and demons bred with humans to help strengthen the species in hope that if this ever happened again, there would be survivors."

Tegan wrapped his arm around his mate and pulled her to his side. "That is why you are needed. Without a strong species to help, humanity will vanish once again."

Decker still wasn't following how he fit into this equation. "I'm no longer human or did you miss that memo?"

"You might be immortal, but you carry human DNA which will be passed on to your children. Humanity will continue, only stronger this time, and magic will be brought back into this world. Just as it was with the first beings who built their homes across this planet."

"Are you saying we can procreate?" Ryder asked. "I thought that was questionable."

Rhea smiled. "Our son, Jacob." She held the child in outstretched arms and Emma was the first to take the baby and fold him into her chest.

"He is beautiful, but how is he going to save us?" she asked the question they all wanted to know. It was said that Tegan and Rhea's son would save the world, but could they wait for him to grow up?

"He has already begun. When he was born, I had a vision of a woman who was round with child. That woman is among the group with Wolfe and she is now pregnant with her first baby sired by one of Wolfe's vampires."

"You have seen her? Where is Wolfe, we haven't been able to get in touch with him," Ryder asked.

"We just came from them to confirm my vision. They are traveling and communication isn't working, but they are well and the girl I saw is healthy," Rhea replied.

"Wait, back up. So, what role exactly does your son play in this?" Ryder asked.

"Jacob is the son of a pure angel." Tegan cast a glance at his mate. "And myself, who carries DNA from both the Maker and Lucifer."

"Ooookay. Not following the DNA lesson here." Decker was fast losing patience.

"Put in simple terms. It has long been prophesied that when a child carrying that DNA was born, he would have the power of procreation. His birth alone brought about the fertility of the female and I assure you others will follow. My son will also be the first to father angelic daughters."

The only daughters an angel was able to father were nephilim that were mothered by humans. Once an angel procreated with another angel, only sons were born. It was a complicated mess Decker didn't really care to know about. He looked at Ryder. "This is too much. I need to walk."

"Are you sure?"

"Yes." Then Decker left the group standing there to discuss whatever. He didn't want to hear anymore. He didn't want to face his demons either, yet his legs carried him down the oh-so-familiar street. To the end of the driveway that led up to the two-story, yellow house. As he stood there, staring at the overgrown bushes that covered half of the living room window, he was bombarded with visions that were enough to shake him to his core. He fisted his hands and forced his legs to continue up the drive. To the front door that he knew wasn't locked.

He twisted the knob and shoved open the door. Mildew and mold assaulted his senses but he pressed on. Carried by the demons inside him because the part of him that held common sense screamed this was going to hurt. Being here would be more painful than anything he'd done in a long time.

Standing in the living room, he took in the dust-covered furniture and the air thick with it as the sunlight streamed in the windows. He should run back out the door he came in, instead he walked to the fireplace mantel and pulled down a picture frame. He wiped his hand over the thick dust to reveal a face that haunted him nightly.

"Sophie." The name caught in his throat.

She stared back at him. Her eyes accusing. Her voice screaming his failure.

He pulled in a deep breath and for the first time since he held her over a year ago. Since she and their unborn daughter died in his arms, he let the tears come.

"YOU NEED TO GO TO HIM," Rhea said, offering to take the baby back.

Emma looked in the direction Decker stormed off in. "I don't think he wants anyone to follow him. Especially me." The pain he had been experiencing was evident and standing there killed her.

"He needs you and his healing cannot begin without you," Tegan said. "Trust me on this one."

She tried to stand taller, but felt so small at the moment. "Okay, if you think I can help." She wasn't even sure how she was going to help Decker fight his demons. Before she was able to think further, she headed in the same direction he'd gone. Walked past houses that had once held love but now likely held horrors. Who knew what happened to those who died? Some would have been buried, but others died where they were. She tried not to think about it.

Emma noticed a door open on the next house and figured that must be where Decker went. Steeling her resolve to help him, she walked across what was left of the lawn until she reached the front porch. One boot in front of the other, she made her way up the stairs and across the wooden planks that creaked with each step until she reached the door. Agony overcame her and she instantly knew the emotion wasn't her own. It did, however, fill her eyes with unshed tears. Decker hurt that bad? She leaned into the doorway, and that's when she spotted him. Head down, shoulders hunched forward, and he clutched a picture frame. He looked totally defeated, and it broke her.

"You don't belong here." His words were guttural.

She ignored them and walked inside. The mark on her wrist burned, and she tried to rub it, hoping to ease the pain. No such luck. Instead, she walked to where he stood. Both afraid and needing to be close to him.

"Decker, I know it's none of my business but I want to help."

"Unless you're planning to drive a stake in my heart—which I don't think will kill me—you can't help me."

"Maybe if you talked to me?" She glanced at the photo he clutched so tight his knuckles were pale. It was Decker and a beautiful woman, and they were both touching her very pregnant stomach. "Oh Decker, I assume she was your wife?" She didn't want to share that Ace had already given her some of the story. It was Decker's to tell.

"Sophie. We were so happy to welcome our first child."

Her heart cracked.

"I was on a mission when Arsenia found me and turned me against my will." He never looked up from the picture. "I stayed away until my blood lust was under control then I came home." He finally looked up but not at Emma. Instead, he hugged the photo to his chest.

"I told Sophie what had happened and she became so frightened she packed her things and left." He worked his jaw. "I gave her a week, hoping she'd come back to me but then the Red Death hit. I tracked her. Found her." Finally, he looked at her and the pain in his eyes...

Her heart shattered.

"She was alone in a crappy motel and sick. By the time I got to her she was on death's door. I held her while she tried to fight me. With her last breath, she told me I had brought this on. Called me the devil then died in my arms. I lost them both that day." He set the photo on the mantel.

"I'm so sorry." She moved closer and laid her hand on his chest. "It wasn't your fault."

"She died thinking I was a monster."

"I'm sure she no longer thinks that. She loved you and would never want you to hurt this bad. People often react badly when frightened or angry." She had no idea what else to say. How to help him move on.

"Part of me knows that. Sophie was the kindest person I know." He actually gave a little smile. "You remind me of her. Your kindness and always wanting to help."

She wasn't sure if that reminder was good or bad. "The deal you made?"

"Tegan promised I could be with Sophie if I helped him. It was a lie. I won't be getting my redemption."

"I think you have. Just in a different way." She stepped back, feeling like Decker needed time alone. His emotions were a bit calmer than when she'd entered the house. "I'll leave you. I think you need some time here."

He gave a nod. "We can't stay here. In this town."

"I understand. I'll ask Jag to help me find another gate." Then she turned and left, feeling for the first time Decker might be finding some peace. Perhaps this was the best medicine ever. Coming to this place.

CHAPTER FOURTEEN

"SOPHIE NEVER MEANT THOSE WORDS."

Decker faced the strange female with pure white wings. "Who are you?"

"Eva. I'm a guardian and it was I who took your wife to her new life." She stepped closer. "It was also I who sent Emma back to the living."

While he was grateful for Emma being alive, he had so many questions. "Is Sophie happy?"

"Yes, as is your daughter. It was Sophie who begged for you to have a second chance."

"I don't understand."

"She knew her words hurt you and regretted them the moment they came out. It was she who chose Emma."

"I don't understand, and how do I know you speak the truth?"

"I'm a guardian, not a liar. True mates are chosen by higher powers and Sophie helped pick yours. She has moved on. Now you should too. It's time to let her go." The angel spread her wings and gave them a slight flip. "Don't take for granted what's in front of you. You can never go back, but you can always move forward." Then Eva faded away. It was almost like she was never there, except for the white feather that floated to the floor.

He looked back at the picture of him and Sophie. She wasn't angry with him. Could he forgive himself? Did she want him to be here and happy with someone else? He looked at the marking on his wrist. Was this because of her request?

So much to think about.

He bent over and picked up the feather, tucking it into his pocket before he headed for the door. With the soft click of the latch, he locked his past away. The only other item he took was a small locket he'd given Sophie on their second wedding anniversary. It held a photo of them and was now snug in his pocket. He would always love her, but she wanted him to move on. Forgive himself for what happened. It was the Sophie he knew and loved, and the thought brought back the many talks they had long into the night. Being a Navy Seal meant his life was at risk and he made her promise if anything happened to him, she would move on. Would love again and have a happy life.

She'd made him make the same promise.

As he walked across the overgrown lawn, he turned back and looked at the house. At the porch swing he'd installed because Sophie had wanted one so badly. They had spent many evenings on that swing watching the children play in the quiet street.

"I need a sign, Sophie. Something to tell me you want me to move on." He waited. The air still around him when the swing suddenly began to move. For a brief moment, he felt her, the marking on his wrist burned and then she was gone. He looked at his marking again. Decker still wasn't ready for what it meant, but he was a step closer. He could now openly admit his attraction to Emma and that it was more than sexual without a shit-ton of guilt.

He turned back around and walked to the street. Not once did he stop to look back. He had to put his past behind him. Sophie wanted that. She had always wanted him to help those less fortunate and she would want him to help humanity survive. Sophie would want him to make sure the children were safe. He thought of the child with them and wondered if any others survived.

Out there.

Alone.

As he headed down the street to catch up with the others, his resolve grew. He was Arsenia's first. He held powers he still didn't know how to use. Kept them tucked away because he didn't want to be what he was. Now, he would bring them out and rain Hell down on any who threatened those around him. Light shown on the horizon for humanity. A female was with child and they needed to all come together to make sure that baby was born. Was protected. They would face whatever this new world unleashed on them and they would survive.

All of them.

When he finally caught up with the others, Emma seemed excited.

"We found another gate. Jag says it goes to a place south of a big city, near a river."

"Then we should check it out." He looked around. "Tegan left?"

"Yes, he was gone when I got back." She moved closer. "You okay?" she whispered.

"Better. Thanks." He didn't know what else to say. Things between them were difficult. How did he say when she was this close to him, he wanted to wrap himself around her and never let go? Bury himself inside her. Claim every inch of her and forget the world outside had gone to hell. He still had guilt for wanting her. Was afraid of what it might bring for both of them. Did he deserve to start his life over?

"Let's head out then," Ryder said.

Emma walked to a tree, and suddenly another gate opened. Ryder and Kayla went through, followed by Jag. Emma waited.

"I'll follow you," he said, and she looked at him with worry still in her eyes. "I promise I'll be right behind you."

"Okay." Then she was gone, and he kept his word and stepped

into the gate. On the other side he walked into an open area with thick forest to one side and what looked like possible open fields in the distance. His exceptional hearing picked up running water. The sounds of a river.

"This is promising," Kayla said.

"How about we split up? Kayla and I will go check out the source of water and you guys head the other direction?" Ryder proposed.

"Sound plan. Hopefully, we won't run into a rogue," Decker replied.

Jag spoke up. "You have Emma and myself. Perhaps I should go with Ryder and Kayla just in case. Emma is capable of using her magic as long as I'm in the same vicinity as her."

"I like that plan." Ryder started to lead his team away, and Decker motioned to Emma.

"Shall we?"

"Sure, I..." she touched her temple and began to sway.

"Emma!" Decker caught her before she hit the ground. She looked up at him, her eyes dim with pain. "What's wrong?"

"I-I don't know. I don't feel so good. Hot."

That's when he noticed sweat beads on her forehead. Her skin way too warm. He searched for his mental link with Ryder.

Ryder, I need Jag here now. Something's wrong with Emma.

On our way.

"Hold on, Emma. We'll figure this out." He looked skyward and sent out a mental prayer laced with a threat. *Tegan, you son of a bitch, I'm not doing this again.*

VOICES SPOKE IN THE DISTANCE. So far away, Emma thought they were a dream until she forced her eyes open to find herself surrounded by white walls. "It's hot in here." Her throat was scratchy and desert dry.

Kayla helped her to sit and offered a drink of water. After she took a long sip, she leaned back against several pillows and wondered how she'd gotten back in the infirmary.

"You have a fever," Kayla said.

"How high?"

"I checked you an hour ago, and it was a hundred and two."

That explained why her muscles ached and her head felt like someone was doing jumping jacks on it. She licked her dry lips. How had she gone from fine one minute to sicker than a dog the next? Her first thought was the Red Death. Had she finally contracted it? To her knowledge it started like a common cold. She didn't have sniffles or a runny nose. Fever wasn't a symptom of the plague. She wasn't fond of the idea of her heart exploding. A nasty side effect of the Red Death and how it had gotten its name.

"Jag is outside waiting. He says he may be able to find out what's wrong with you. Some kind of magic thing, I guess. Shall I send him in?"

"Okay." She wondered where Decker had gone. Was he waiting outside too or had he walked away?

"Decker's busy tearing a path into the floor outside from his non-stop pacing." Kayla smiled. "He cares about you even if he is too stubborn to admit it."

She tried to smile, but even that hurt. If she was really needed here to help the survivors and Decker, getting sick didn't make sense. Maybe this was a simple flu bug. God, she hoped it wasn't another round of plague. Just as her mind started to dive into a pit of despair, the door opened and Decker poked his head in.

"Can Jag and I come in?"

"Yes, please." God, it even hurt to talk.

They both entered the room and closed the door behind them. Decker moved off to the side, while Jag came closer.

"If you don't mind, I think I might know what the problem is. To be sure, I need to touch you."

"Please. I feel like absolute hell."

Jag stood on one side of the bed and placed his hand on her abdomen. Decker growled.

"Seriously? You can just zip it over there." Emma wasn't in any mood for Decker and his bullshit. He had no claim on her, though every fiber of her being wished he did. It was getting more difficult to be near him. Emma's insides warmed as she felt a tug where Jag's hand was.

"What is it you're doing?"

"As I suspected. Being a witch who just came into her power, you were a bit overloaded. I'm simply bleeding some off and you should start to feel better."

Now that he mentioned it, she was feeling much better. "Wow, that was quick. It's like I was never sick." Jag stepped back and Emma sat up, ready to face the world once more. "Will this happen again?"

"It could, but now that we know, I can keep a better eye on you and either have you bleed off the excess yourself or take it from you. Once you grow stronger, it should become less frequent."

"Thank you, Jag. You've been so much help to all of us. It's still hard to believe everything that's happened."

"Just remember, if you start to feel slightly ill, make sure you seek me out."

"I will."

OUTSIDE EMMA'S ROOM, Decker stopped Jag. "What the hell are you hiding? You lied to her in there, yet you also spoke the truth."

Jag stopped and faced him. "She did have excess power that made her ill. However, I'm only her conduit to the magic. I'm her familiar and can only take so much of her power. Emma proves to become a powerful witch and at some point, she will have more magic than I can take from her. She may destroy both me and herself."

"What? How do we fix this?" Having Emma sick in that bed

caused him more distress than he cared for. Once again, he'd been left helpless to do anything to fix what was wrong.

"Do you care for her?"

"Of course. I like Emma, she's—"

"No." Jag cut him off. "I mean, do you have real feelings for her? Obviously, by your actions you can't stand another man near her. Your mating mark, it burns you, doesn't it?"

Decker rubbed his thumb over his wrist yet didn't answer.

"She's a ticking bomb, and you'd better figure out what's in your head and heart, because if she doesn't bond with her mate soon, she might destroy us all. You were chosen to be hers for a reason, I can see that now. The power you feel deep inside of you that you're not sure what it is? It is her. She will feed that, and you will take her excess. You are meant to complement each other but you need to bond."

"Nothing like trying to force my hand on this matter. Fucking fate. Who decides this bullshit anyway? The Almighty? You said earlier that it was decided by a higher power."

"Not him."

"The Maker then?" She was the Almighty's daughter and in charge of the angelic realm.

"Not even her."

"Then who the fuck is it?" Decker was losing what tiny speck of patience he had left.

"The angels are the ones who are trying to protect humanity. For the same reasons you and the other primordials were chosen, a match was made for each of you to ensure the best chances of survival."

Decker wasn't sure he was processing this information correctly. "Angels? The same ones who aren't here now helping us?"

Jag sighed. "Because you don't see it, doesn't mean it's not happening. They foresaw the possibility of the Gate of the Gods being opened by Lucifer and knew the tragedy that would follow. The waking of Arsenia and the ones she chose to turn was not a coincidence. It was the will of lesser gods and angels who wish to keep this world alive."

"Why not simply tell us this?"

"Because they are not supposed to interfere. I tell you this so you can understand what's at stake. If the Almighty catches wind of this, he could destroy every lesser god and angel that breathes. If my goddess is destroyed, then so are all those who carry her DNA." Jag stared at him.

"As well as those who carry angel DNA."

"Now you're catching on."

"Everything in this world and every realm around it would perish."

"Exactly. They can only give you a fighting chance and that is what they have done. It's up to you to take it." Jag turned and walked away, leaving Decker with a lot to think about and a difficult choice to make.

CHAPTER FIFTEEN

EMMA HAD BUSIED herself packing up what medical supplies were left so they could begin the transport to their new location. Jag had taken a team back, and it was decided that the second location in Kentucky looked like a good place to relocate. Ryder had even been able to get ahold of Shade before he headed out of Mexico and told him to stay put if possible. The hope was Emma could find a gate that led to them and move Shade's people to Kentucky. Jag taught Emma how to meditate and call on the magic of Gaia to show her where the lines of power—otherwise called ley lines—were located. She did have to be outside in order to see the map and right now could only find it in the dark. Decker had insisted he be there to watch her back while she was outside the compound. She looked forward to that time. In between her trying to figure out the map and her magical power, they talked. She learned about his childhood and how he had gone into the Navy after high school graduation. She also shared her past and felt like they were growing closer.

She placed the last of the bandages in a box when he walked in the room. Decker always had a way of taking charge of the space he occupied. Or maybe it was her simply admiring that killer body.

Either way, every time he was near her, it was a battle not to wrap herself around him and lick him from head to toe.

"How's it going?"

"Good. This is the last box." She folded it shut, grateful for the conversation that might get her head out of Decker's pants.

"You feeling okay?"

"I'm fine. How about you?" she lied, because she needed to get laid.

"Looking forward to getting everyone settled in our new location. Ryder wants to know if you're any closer to locating a gate to Mexico?"

She sighed. "I'm not sure. Maybe I need Jag to help me. I mean he is my familiar."

"He's manning the gate right now while they move stuff. I can go out with you if you want to try again? Maybe there's something I can do to help you."

"I'm not sure how you can help, but I'm willing to try anything at this point. I can see the ley lines, I just can't figure out where they go or how they're connected."

"We can go now if you want."

She gave a nod. "Sounds good." She grabbed a jacket from the top of an exam table and slipped it on. The air was still brisk at night here in the mountains. "Okay." She moved past him, her body aching from the heat he emitted and something else she felt.

"When was the last time you fed?" She was hoping he hadn't taken from one of the other women. The little monster with the green eyes inside her wouldn't be happy.

"The last time you fed me."

She whirled to face him. "It's been too long. Why do you wait and place yourself in danger?"

"Because I'm pretty damn sure if I feed from you, I won't stop there."

Her face heated and the flash of fire went straight to her sex. "I won't ask you to stop." It was all she could do to not throw herself at him right now. They had work to do. He stared at her for a long time before speaking.

"Let's go find that gate. Jag had a suggestion for us to try." He headed for the compound's entrance.

They walked in silence. It took them a good ten minutes to get outside where they found a clear night. The wind was calm, and the stars sparkled like tiny diamonds. It was easy to forget the world was in a mess right now.

"This way."

Decker led her up a hill and when they reached the top, she found a blanket spread out. He moved to the center and sat, knees bent, legs open. He patted the spot in front of him.

"Sit here. Jag suggested this position might help you use me as your power source."

"Really?" She moved between his thighs, her back to his chest. The only thing contact with him was going to do was send her libido soaring and her mood on a downward spiral. How was she supposed to concentrate with his erection pressing into her backside? When she would have scooted further away, he pulled her closer. Pinned her in with his powerful thighs then placed his hands on her shoulders and began to massage away the tension in her upper body. Of course, it only caused more in her lower half.

Fuck my life!

She needed sex and the only man she wanted was right here torturing her. This was never going to work. As she started to protest, he pressed his mouth to her neck.

She gasped. "Decker."

"Shhh. Let me help you."

He peppered light kisses and suckled the sensitive spot until she was on the edge. All she could think about was sweet release and if she didn't get it, someone was going to die.

Slowly.

He continued to kiss her while his other hand slid underneath her shirt. His thumb brushed the underside of her breast, and she nearly melted into him. She was way too hot and wished they were both naked.

Nothing happened. So much for magic when you wanted it to do your bidding.

He pinched her nipple.

She moaned. "More."

His other hand had managed to free the button on her jeans and lower the zipper. His fingers were already slipping between her panties and skin.

She was going to spontaneously combust.

He slid a finger into her folds. "You're so wet."

"Your fault," she croaked.

"I will fix that." And on his last word, he plunged a finger inside her.

"God, yes." She spread her legs to give him better access even though she still had her jeans on. He slipped in a second finger and she leaned further into him. Pressure built, and the world spun around her. Such sweet bliss was on the horizon and she was on the edge waiting to topple over. His thumb brushed her clit as he sank his fangs into her neck.

Her world tilted.

Color exploded behind her lids as she cried out, certain the entire compound heard her. She didn't care as her climax carried her on a wave of euphoria that crested then swept her away again. Time stood still until Decker finally retracted his fangs and licked the puncture so it would heal. Her body was limp. Muscles forgot how to function and all she could do was lie on his chest, feeling the beat of his heart against her back.

"Decker, what are we doing?" Somehow, she managed words, then shuffled her tired body around to face him.

"Taking the first step." He shoved up the sleeve on his shirt and showed his wrist. The partial marking was pulsing the same color, and energy as the ley lines.

She swallowed, then met his gaze. "Are you sure you want to do this?"

"I know things between us have been... well, strained. That's on me. I need to let go of my past and wake up to the present."

"So, you've let go then?"

"I'll always carry Sophie with me, but she would want me to move on."

She reached out and took his hand in hers. "Your wife was a big part of your life. You loved her and I would expect her to always be with you."

He squeezed her hand. "I've fought my attraction for you from the day I walked into this compound. Told myself that you would be nothing more than a quick fling to ease an ache. Yet, I find myself obsessed with your safety. Where you are and the thought of another man touching, you makes me want to rip their head off. You are on my mind every second I'm awake and in my dreams every night. I'm not human anymore, Emma. I'm something I still don't understand and at times it scares even me."

She touched his cheek. "I'm scared too. I mean, I carry some kind of magic that I can't even comprehend. Does that mean I'm no longer human as well? I've no idea what being a witch means. I only know that I hate being without you. I feel like..." She looked up at the sky. "Like part of me is missing, if that makes sense."

"It does. Now how about we find those gates?"

She gave a nod and realized her vision was clearer, as was her mind. The ley lines more vibrant in the night's sky and each one held a symbol that would unlock its location.

JAG HAD BEEN RIGHT. Clearing Emma's mind by easing her sexual energy had allowed her to gain better control of her powers. Him drinking from her had darkened his marking and brought them closer together. Things were different. He felt more connected to her and it stirred something powerful inside him. Emma was also positive she knew how to jump gates and get to Mexico.

It had taken them a week to move most of their supplies from site R to their new location in Kentucky. They had no idea what the town's name had once been before as the sign was gone, but someone suggested they rename it Independence. It seemed fitting since they were starting over and the American flag still flew in front of the small city building. Many took it as a sign.

The town appeared to have everything they required. Water, forest, and there was wildlife to hunt as well as land to farm. There were homes that, once cleaned up, could be inhabited. Of course, there was no electricity or hot water, but they would figure that out. They had candles and lanterns for now and warm weather. Someone had also discovered a greenhouse on the edge of town. While over-grown, there were seeds they hoped proved to be good. A team of people were busy cleaning it up and getting ready to plant vegetables. Decker hadn't seen this much happiness and hope in the eyes and actions of the people around him since he'd arrived at site R.

"Decker?" Emma slid in next to him. "Kayla is ready to try to open a portal to the gate we need to get us to Mexico."

He nodded, then faced her. "I've got our team. Besides you, Kayla, Ryder and myself, Carlos and Hunter are coming along. Jag stays here to help guard the others."

"Agreed. He says I won't need him for this." She stepped closer, touched his cheek, then kissed him. While it was a quick kiss, it was full of passion and Emma. A blue spark crossed their lips that sent a tingle between them. He was starting to get used to the odd power current that seemed to spark when they touched. It was Emma's magic, and it even felt like her.

"He also said you can help with my magic should I need it. You seem to be getting pretty good at that."

True. He'd learned how to take Emma's excess power and filter it through himself. The more he drank from her, the more connected he became to her. Also, the darker his marking got. It was still only an infinity symbol, the heart missing until they bonded. Emma's mark never changed. She still bore the heart missing the infinity, which meant she was still mortal, unlike him. Their bond would not be completed—at least as far as he knew—until they had sex. So far, he'd only taken care of Emma's needs and left his own until his balls were now blue. It wasn't as if she didn't offer to take care of him. He was afraid of where it would take them and he wasn't ready yet to bond them together forever. He'd checked with Jag, who was keeping an eye on Emma's magic, and so far, she was in no danger of combusting. For now, what he was doing seemed to be helping. Apparently, orgasms were helpful to a witch.

"We'll meet the rest of the team by the river bank." He took her hand and led her to the rendezvous point. A few minutes later, they met up with the rest of the crew and Kayla was there ready to get to work.

"I make no promises, but Emma showed me on her ley line map where we need to go and I think I can open a portal to at least get us close." She crossed her fingers. "I hope."

Ryder slipped his arm around Kayla and pulled her close, kissing her cheek. "You've got this."

Kayla smiled. "Thanks." Then she closed her eyes and for several seconds, Decker wondered if she was going to be able to do it, but then the familiar portal flashed open in front of them.

"Okay, Carlos and Hunter go through first," Decker said and his men stepped into the black mass of spiraling white lights. After a few minutes, Decker was able to get a message from Carlos that all appeared good. Time for them to head into the unknown.

CHAPTER SIXTEEN

EMMA LOOKED around her and tried to get her bearings. The air was thick with humidity, making breathing difficult. She wouldn't complain though. The warmth—moist as it was—was welcome on her skin.

"Damn, this remind you of anything, Ryder?" Decker asked.

"We spent many missions in jungles like this one." Ryder looked around. "The sounds mean life still exists, at least for the wildlife."

Spider monkeys swung from the treetops. Their calls of alarm carried across the forest and caused a rustle of trees for miles. They had likely not seen a human since the Red Death.

"Which way, Emma?" Decker asked.

"I need a moment." She closed her eyes and tried to drown out the surrounding sounds until she was able to pull in a faint hum. It was the magic she was looking for, or so she hoped. Opening her eyes, she turned and pointed. "This way."

Ryder started out front, cursing at the thick forest in front of them.

"Let me." Emma moved forward, Decker hot on her heels. He was never more than a few steps behind her when they were on a mission. She tried to forget he was so close that he literally sent electrical pulses across her skin. Instead, she concentrated on instinct. Stretching her arms out, she sent a mental vision of a clear path.

"Damn!" Kayla exclaimed. "Your magic gets more impressive each time I see it."

A path began to clear. Brush parted, and Emma was able to see for several yards in front of her. When she started to walk forward, Decker was quick to stop her.

"I go first." He already had a high-powered rifle ready to shoot anything that posed a danger. "Don't forget, I'm used to missions like this one."

She would gladly allow him to go first. Jungles were definitely not something she was familiar with, so she stepped aside, then followed. "I'll let you know when to stop."

They moved down a narrow path, trees blocked the sun and cast eerie shadows around them. Sounds from above and on all sides caused Emma's pulse to race. She kept expecting something to jump out and attack them. So far that hadn't happened. The magical pulse she followed finally started to get stronger.

"I think we're getting closer. I can feel an energy spike."

"Thank god, because I was beginning to wonder how many miles away I'd brought us," Kayla said, wiping sweat from her brow. "Not to mention the fact a cat has been following us."

"I sense it too," Ryder said.

"A cat?" Emma scanned the thick brush around them, but wasn't able to see a damn thing. She wondered why she didn't sense it. "Decker?"

"Yep. It's followed us for at least a half mile or so."

"Jesus, why didn't anyone say anything?"

"Because so far it only seems curious, however, I think it's time to send that cat a message. Excuse me a moment." Kayla slipped behind a tree and a second later stepped out as a jaguar. It was still incredible to see her friend shift into the large black cat. Emma wasn't sure if she would ever get used to it. Kayla was beautiful. Long and sleek, she carried the thick muscles of a large cat, and when she moved, it was with a graceful power.

"We should keep moving," Ryder said.

"What's she doing?" Emma tried to see, but lost sight of the cat.

"Going to let the other cat know she's done with being stalked." Ryder grinned. "My mate's bad-ass."

Kayla might be exactly that, but it didn't stop Emma from worrying about her friend. She followed Decker though, and they continued on the trail for several minutes before they came to a clearing. The entire team stopped short and stared. Spread out before them was a vast open grassy area, but it was what took center stage that caught her attention. One of Mexico's Mayan pyramids.

"Amazing," she whispered. It was hard to believe she was standing in front of such a national treasure.

"It's not vacant," Decker said as he came alongside of her. "Get ready to wield your bag of magic tricks." He looked at her. "Do you know where the gate is?"

She swallowed and suspected Decker must detect demons or had the ancient people come back to life like they had in Machu Picchu? Neither was good in her opinion. "I'm getting a huge power spike from the pyramid itself."

"Great, any bets the fucking gate is inside?" Ryder asked.

"Why would it be anywhere else?" Decker pointed out. "Did Jag mention anything about these gates being guarded?"

"No. Not a word," she replied.

"Kayla is coming behind us," Ryder pointed out and Emma expected to see the human Kayla, but instead the sleek cat slipped in next to Ryder who reached down and gave a loving knead to the cat's powerful neck. "There's really nowhere for us to sneak up on whoever is in there."

"I don't suppose you guys know how many there are?" Emma hated not having the same ability to sense things that the vampires did. However... "I have an idea. Not sure if it will work, but since

Kayla is still in cat form, I might be able to see through her eyes. It's a simple spell Jag taught me and won't hurt Kayla at all."

The cat moved from Ryder next to Emma. She knew that even as a wild animal, Kayla understood every word they said. She placed one hand on the top of the cat's large head, closed her eyes and asked Gaia to give her sight. A minute later, Kayla bounded across the open grass and Emma saw everything with new eyes.

"Wow, this is amazing," she whispered. The world whizzed past as Kayla quickened her pace to a trot. Once she was closer to the temple, she slinked up the stairs and poked her head through the opening. Things appeared gray yet crystal clear. Cats had great night vision.

"What are you seeing?" Decker asked.

"Only darkness right now. She's rounding a corner and holy shit! Demons! Lots of them."

Emma watched, her breath stuck in her lungs while she waited for something. Anything to happen and prayed Kayla didn't get hurt or worse. She'd never forgive herself if anything happened to any of the team. She was the one who had led them into danger, even if it was to save Shade and his people. Her panic must have broken the spell, because she lost Kayla's sight.

"I can't see what's going on anymore."

A demon head rolled down the stairs, and that was their cue to make a run for the ruins. Before Emma was able to think about moving, she was swept off her feet and found herself over the shoulder of one hulking vampire.

"Sorry, Emma, but I can run faster than you and there's no way I'm leaving you behind." He managed to fire off his rifle at a demon that appeared in front of the ruins.

"Damn it, put me down. I can't fight like this." She understood what he was trying to do, but she had the power of magic and a few tricks up her sleeve. Fire being one of them.

DECKER SET Emma on her feet, but he despised letting her go. There wasn't much choice, however, demons were coming at them from the ruins and he had to shoot to knock them down. They probably should have brought backup, but he sensed there weren't that many close by.

He fired his rifle while Emma summoned her magic. He felt the pull of it inside him. She was gearing up to do something he hoped was big. He wanted to get this mission done and head back with Shade and his people to their new camp. They had a lot of work ahead of them. Plus, he was done tip-toeing around this mating thing. He wanted the female in front of him—about to unleash her own kind of hell—to be his.

His marking burned as Emma pulled more power within herself and seconds later, a blast of fire erupted in the center of three demons who'd come out to fight. It was glorious to witness what Emma was capable of. Decker knew she would become as dangerous as him. Maybe even more so.

Kayla, still in her cat form, rushed out the opening and down the steps.

"Kayla gives the all clear," Ryder said and moved forward. Kayla rushed back into the forest, probably to shift. It was something Decker had noticed she liked to do privately whenever possible.

"Let's go," Decker said as he looked at Emma. "That was a pretty cool thing you did, my little witch."

"Thanks." She grinned and started for the ruins. "I can feel the gate's energy."

Once they were inside, Emma led them through a maze of rooms until they reached what appeared to be a sacrificial table. Several steps above it sat a carved stone throne. From the looks of it, it had been pilfered long ago. There were gouges and pits indicating robbers had taken any gold and jewels laid into the stone.

"There it is." Emma rushed up the stairs and ducked behind the throne. For the first time, Decker saw a faint light.

"I think I see it." He moved in beside her. "There?" He pointed.

"Yes!" Emma almost jumped up and down with excitement. "I can't believe you can see it."

"I catch a faint light. If I wasn't looking for it, I would miss it."

"Hurry." She placed her hand over the invisible lock. A surge of power rushed across his skin and the gate opened.

"Ryder first," Decker said and his friend didn't hesitate. In he went, followed by Kayla, Emma and Decker and his men were last. When he stepped out the other side, it looked much like where they had come from, except the ruins were a bit different.

"There is definitely energy here. I can feel it crackle across my skin," Ryder said as he rubbed his arms.

"It's the same feeling I get from the ley lines. It has a magical energy to it." Emma looked around. "Really weird."

"According to Shade, he's only about a mile south of these ruins." Decker turned south and studied the landscape. "This way. I can feel a pull in that direction. Do you feel it, Ryder?"

"I do. Like a magnet to brethren. Let's move before something goes wrong."

"Agreed." Decker took Emma's hand, and they headed in the direction of the third primordial vampire.

They hadn't even made it halfway, when Shade emerged from the trees, rifle resting on his shoulder. "Am I glad to see your ugly mugs."

"Thank goodness," Emma breathed a verbal sigh of relief.

"My people are right behind me. Shit's packed and they are ready to leave." Shade scanned the area, and his gaze landed on Emma. He moved closer and Decker tried not to growl. He was not going to become more of a dickhead than he was already feeling.

"I'm guessing you're Emma. Thanks for coming for us."

"Yes, but how did you know I was the one?"

"Because Decker growled when my gaze landed on you." Shade grinned.

"You're a fucktard," Decker said. "Now, can we get the hell out of here?"

Shade only laughed. "*Cabro*, your undies are in a bunch again. Besides, you two smell the same." He tapped his nose. "Being a vampire has ramped up my sense of smell."

Emma turned a nice shade of pink. "Do I detect a slight Spanish accent?"

Decker's mood soured further with the excitement in her words.

"Yes. I was born in Costa Rica, my parents moved to America when I was sixteen." He turned. "Ah, here they come. We can go now." Several men carrying firearms moved in with the women behind them. There was an endless line of people.

"Fucking finally!" Decker started to move out, making sure Emma was behind him.

"Shade, we have found a nice community back in Kentucky. The people are back there now getting things set up. I know they are looking forward to increasing our numbers. Those damn rogues are exhausting," Ryder said.

"Tell me. They've been quiet here in recent weeks which makes me damn edgy," Shade responded, moving next to Ryder. "How far to this gate thing?"

"Not far, but we did encounter demons at our first jump. It took two gates and portal to get to you."

"Damn. Well, we're armed so the demons can go fuck themselves."

If only. These excursions were making Decker twitchy. His gut was certain some big shit was about to come down. It was only a matter of what and when.

CHAPTER SEVENTEEN

THEY HAD MANAGED to make it back to camp right at dusk and Emma was thankful when Jag had showed her to a small, one-story house near the river. He'd even managed to set up some lanterns and scored bedding for the queen bed in the master suite. It was a crying shame that the whirlpool tub was a no go. Her aching body sure could use it right now. It had been a long day. When she was about to strip and clean up, the front door opened, and Decker stepped inside.

"Can I come in?"

"Looks to me like you already did."

He closed the door behind him, sending the small living room into a cast of dancing shadows. "I..." He moved closer, placed his hands on her shoulders and started kneading sore muscles.

"Oh lord, don't stop. That feels sooo good." She thought her knees might give out, except he held her up. That was until he leaned in, bringing his lips to her ear and whispered, "I want you, Emma."

Her breathing hitched. "Do you mean what I think you mean?" What a lame question.

"I do. But if we have sex, it will complete our bond." He leaned back to look her in the eyes.

"Is that what you want?" She held her breath. Were they finally going to take the next step?

He slipped his hand upward to touch her cheek. "I know things between us have been complicated, but I'm ready to move on. With you."

"The next step?"

"The next step." He gave a nod.

She was nervous. This was a big deal and meant forever or at least as long as they both lived. She stared into his blue eyes. She cared for this man a great deal. The mark on her wrist tingled. "I'm ready too."

He lifted her, carried her to the bedroom and laid her down. She prayed that this time there would be no interruptions like before. Emma grabbed the hem of her shirt and lifted. As she tried to pull it over her head, Decker took over, catching one of her nipples in his mouth as he rid her of the garment.

She moaned and arched into him. The orgasms he'd been giving her were nice, but she needed him. Wanted to feel him inside her. Craved that connection with him. She reached for his tee and tugged it free of his jeans. He leaned back and ripped it off his body.

Damn, he was glorious in the light of the lantern. She traced her fingers over the ink on his chest, then across his thick biceps. When he grinned, he showed a hint of fang and the heat at her sex increased several degrees. She knew how much pleasure came with feeding him. Not only physical, but emotional as well. She was giving him life and now she was going to share her body to give them both much needed pleasure.

As she started to undo his belt, he leaned down and claimed her mouth. His kiss was demanding, hungry and maybe even a little desperate. His fang pricked her lip, the coppery taste of her blood registered as he suckled her mouth. She worked faster to undo his jeans but wasn't able to get them off. Instead, she reached in and rubbed the tip of his cock. Smoothed his pre-cum over the head. She wanted these jeans off him and now.

Like he had read her mind, he broke the kiss, jumped from the bed and stripped. She managed to do the same, leaving them both naked and wanting. As he knelt on the bed, she reached for him. Slid down until her mouth was level with exactly what she wanted.

She licked the tip.

He moaned and slipped his fingers into her hair. "Tease."

"Not for long." Then she took the entire head into her mouth. Swirled her tongue along the rim before she took him deeper. He tasted so good, and there was part of her that wanted to bring him to release. There was time for that later. This time, she wanted him inside her. Wanted to feel their bodies joined in sweet bliss.

She worked up and down his shaft in a slow, lazy motion, loving the enjoyment on his face. She could look at him all day. Decker deserved this time more than she did. He had paid such a high price. He'd given her pleasure and taken none for himself.

When she thought she had brought him to the edge, he pulled free.

"Enough. It's my turn." He gave a gentle push until she fell back. He spread her legs and dived between them. It started with a gentle kiss to her thigh. With each one, her sex throbbed and her arousal spiked higher. Then he swiped his tongue between her folds.

"Mmm, more."

"I aim to please."

Then he latched onto her clit, his tongue swirled over the nub and she exploded. A violent rush sent her muscles tightening as wave after wave hit her. She dug her fingers into his scalp. Part of her wanted to beg for mercy while the other wanted to beg for more. Finally, he relented and planted a kiss on her swollen flesh then slid up her body. The tip of his cock touched her, and she shifted. Wanting him inside her more than she wanted to breathe.

"I need you," she whispered, hoping he would drive home. She had waited so long for this moment. For him.

Instead, he showed great restraint and slipped the tip in then stopped. She wiggled, but he pinned her hips to the bed.

"It's been too long, angel. I want to enjoy this fully."

"This is a slow torture," she muttered.

"But a beautiful one." He looked at her, and in his eyes, she saw so much desire and it was all for her.

He pressed further, stretched her, and she was thankful he took it slow. It had been so long since she'd been this intimate. She wrapped her arms around his neck and pulled him closer. Kissed him. He opened, and her tongue met the sharp points that filled his mouth.

Heat flooded her core. Why did she find those damn things so sexy? Maybe because it was part of who Decker was. The only way she had ever known him. She'd not know him as the Navy Seal before the Red Death. Only as the tough vampire who was willing to slay demons and rogues as well as protect those weaker than him. He was tough as nails, had mostly kept to himself in the months they had all spent together. Yet, she felt like she had known him most of her life.

He sank in until he was fully inside her. Her hips still pinned to the bed, he took control. Plundered her mouth and demanded her total surrender as he took her to new heights. He ended the kiss, then whispered, "You are mine, little witch." Then he sank his fangs into her neck and drank. The words, the sensations were too much. Emma was in overload as he took all of her and she freely gave. He released his grip on her hips, and she thrust to meet him. The only sounds were of skin on skin and the moans that escaped her as he took her to another level.

His thrusts deepened as he moved faster. Harder. Until it was almost too much to bear. Hanging on the edge, she knew once she toppled it would be intense. Another thrust sent her over. He kissed her neck to seal the wound, and they both cried out as they tumbled together into a sea of pleasure. The sensations strummed her body over and over, seeming like they would never end, but they did. They both floated down from their euphoria.

"Wow. That was amazing," she whispered.

He dipped his head and kissed the tip of her nose. "I can't believe I waited so long."

"My wrist tingles." He leaned back, and she brought her arm up to inspect it. "Damn, that was fast." She now carried the infinity along with the heart.

He looked at his. "Mine changed too." He showed her, and their markings were identical. He closed his eyes. "I feel you." He tapped over his heart. "In here." He laid next to her and pulled her into him.

"I feel it too. It's both odd yet feels right. Like it's always been this way." She kissed his arm.

"Did you hear that they found a clinic down the street? A crew cleaned it up, and it's all ready for you."

Excitement stirred inside her. "No, I had not heard that. Jag led me straight here when we got back. That's wonderful news."

"I have more. Seems there's a female doctor on Shade's team. I didn't find out what she specializes in, but her name is Linda Edwards."

She turned to face him. "Serious?"

"I swear, but there's more. Also seems she has a faint marking on her wrist and so far none of Shade's vampires have a mark."

She pushed herself up. "You think that her and Ace?"

He shrugged and pulled her back down. "No idea, but it's possible."

"How many people do we have now?" She kissed the tattoo on his chest.

"Ryder and his team are doing a head count, but we believe about four hundred. We still have over four men to every woman though."

"That's still not good. How many do you think this town can support?" She worried about food, clothing, shelter and medical supplies.

"We should be good. There's a team going out tomorrow to scout further north and find out what's out there." He traced his fingers across her bottom side, sending heat straight to her sex. The erection that pressed into her belly indicated Decker was as ready as she was.

"Let's forget about the world outside for tonight." She straddled his hips and sank down on his thick shaft.

"I like your plan," he moaned and gripped her ass. This was going to be a most pleasurable night.

DECKER LAID THERE with Emma tucked into his arms. Her breathing indicated she was finally asleep, but he would know it, regardless. Each time they'd made love, their bond grew stronger. His marking had finally stopped burning after the first time, and now he realized he was able to pin-point his mate's exact location.

His mate.

The words were still foreign to him, yet they seemed to fit. Everything about Emma fit. The way her body curved next to his. And when he was inside her, it was as if she were made for him. Just the thought of being in her stirred his cock, but he pushed those thoughts away. Emma might be immortal now, but she still needed rest.

A banging sounded at the door and he was sorely tempted to ignore it, but the sound increased and Emma stirred.

"Stay put. I'll go deal with whoever is on the other side."

"Don't kill them," she mumbled.

He'd consider her request as he tugged on jeans and headed for the door. Whipping it open. "What?" He stared at one of Shade's humans.

"S-sorry to bother you, but Dr. Edwards has requested the nurse's assistance. We have a sick patient."

"The clinic?"

"Yes. She said to tell her this might be a quarantine."

"Fuck. She'll be right there." Decker slammed the door and headed back to Emma, who was already out of bed and pulling on her clothes.

"I heard. Damn it!" She pulled a shirt over her head. "Maybe it's just a normal virus."

"There's nothing normal anymore." This news made his skin crawl. "I'll walk you to the clinic."

"Thanks." She grabbed a bag that sat in the corner. "Ready."

He took her bag and slung it over his shoulder, then grabbed her hand and gave the marking on her wrist a gentle kiss. The small gesture brought a smile to her face, which in turn made him happy. When was the last time he'd had that feeling? Rather than dwell, he opened the door and led Emma into the morning sun. It appeared to be a perfect Kentucky morning for mid-April. Unfortunately, his instincts told him shit was about to go down.

He walked the five blocks to the clinic as fast as Emma could go. When they reached the front door, two guards stood on either side. Decker reached for his mental link to Ryder.

Ryder, did you stage the guards at the clinic?

That was me being safe. Shade responded. Before Decker had gone to Emma last night, he and Ryder had exchanged blood with Shade, so now all three had a link to each other.

Good thinking. There was no reason to infect anyone else. Flu or not. Best to be safe. One of the guards stopped them.

"Nurse Torres?" he asked, stepping closer and Decker let out a low growl. The other vampire took a step back. "Sorry, sir."

"Yes, I'm her, but call me Emma."

"Yes, ma'am, uh, Emma. You can go in, but sir, you have to stay outside until the doctor clears everyone." The younger guard pulled back his shoulders.

Before Emma could walk inside, Decker pulled her close and kissed her. Deep and long until her knees nearly gave way. Finally, he released her and handed her the bag. Then he looked at both men.

"Anything happens to her, I will personally tear your heads off. Got that?"

"Decker! No reason to be such a brute."

He shoved out his wrist so his marking showed. "Emma is my life now. I'm trusting her care to both of you."

The young guards nodded. "We will guard her with our lives. Sir."

"Send for me if you need anything." He kissed her cheek then sent her inside. Once the door was closed behind her, he once again stared down the two shaking vampires before him.

"Are you the only two here?" He sensed others, but was testing them.

"No, sir. We have two more men stationed at the back door."

"See to it that they also receive my message."

The guard straightened. "Yes, sir!" Then he saluted, indicating he had also been military. Good, Shade had chosen well and now Decker had work to do. He planned to help Ryder and Shade come up with a plan to secure this town. It wasn't going to be easy, but they would make it work. They had no choice. People needed to feel like life was going in a semi-normal direction again.

CHAPTER EIGHTEEN

EMMA STEPPED INSIDE and a female voice called out, "Grab the gear by the door and we're in the last room."

She looked at a chair and found a gown, mask and gloves and quickly pulled them on as she walked down the narrow hall. When she reached the end, she stuck her head in and found a tall. slender woman with a long blonde ponytail dressed in the same mask and gown as herself.

"Dr. Edwards, I'm Emma."

The woman flashed weary green eyes at her. "Emma, please call me Linda. I think we are way past formalities in this world."

"Okay. So what's going on?" She recognized Hunter sitting on the exam table, sweat dripping off his face. This was not a good sign.

Linda waved her inside. "I assume you know Hunter?"

"Yes, he's one of Decker's vampires. What's going on?"

"He woke up with stomach pains and then threw up. He now has a fever of a hundred and one."

"He's a vampire. They aren't supposed to get sick." She moved closer. "Or so I assumed. Do you still have the sun allergy?"

He nodded. "Yeah. I had to take cover in order to get here."

If ever a man looked like shit, he did now. Her concern grew. "Do you think this might be another round of plague?"

Linda nodded and grabbed a glass of water. "Drink this, you're dehydrated. It might be, but who the hell knows. We can't take any chances though. I'm calling for a quarantine of anyone who has come into contact with Hunter over the last week."

"That's a lot of people, Doc," Hunter said.

"I know. It seems excessive, but I don't want to leave anything to chance." She took the empty glass from him and set it on the table. "We have some lab equipment here so I'd like you to take a sample of blood for me. Meantime, I'm sending word that we need a medical tent out back."

"On it." Emma moved in while Linda left the room. She grabbed the items needed from the tray sitting on the counter. "You look awful. How do you feel?" She tied off the band to his arm. "Make a fist and squeeze."

"Like hell."

"Does Decker know you're the one here? He didn't mention it to me." She tapped his vein, then stuck the needle. Blood rushed into the tube, and she undid the band.

"No. I heard him outside making threats. You two official now, I hear. Congrats."

She let out a laugh. "Thanks. I think." She pulled the needle free. He clotted and healed instantly. "Well, at least you still have your healing abilities." She labeled the two vials she'd taken and slipped them into the tray. "Lie back and rest. I'll see what the doc wants to do next."

She left the room in search of the lab. It wasn't hard to find. The clinic was small. A reception desk, six chairs in the waiting room and from what she saw, three exam rooms. An office that must have been for the doctor and a small lab in the very back.

"Here you go." She looked around at the old equipment.

"I know, it's not much, but it's all we got."

"Umm, you do know that we came here from site R?"

Linda shook her head. "I heard the term, but have no idea what it means."

Emma gasped. "Linda, it's an old military bunker deep in a mountain. The lab there is..." she spread her arms and glanced around. "Far superior to this and we can go back there."

The woman's eyes grew bigger. "Why didn't someone tell me this? We can quarantine there?"

"Absolutely. It only takes us a matter of minutes to get there." An idea hit her. "Hunter can communicate with Decker telepathically. I'll ask him to have Decker come back here."

"Good idea. He will have to go into quarantine, anyway."

Emma headed back into the exam room to find Hunter had followed her orders and was lying down. It didn't look very comfortable though, his large frame on a short, narrow table. "Hey."

He sat up. "Done already?"

"No. But I was wondering if you can reach Decker and ask him to come back here?" She gave Hunter a brief overview of their idea to go back to site R.

He gave a nod. "It's done. He will be here soon, but you'll have to explain what's going on. My head is pounding."

Her concern grew. "When did that start?"

"After you left."

She grabbed the thermometer and placed it in his ear. One hundred and two. "Damn, it's going up." She'd kill for an ice pack. "I'll be back." She rushed from the room and on her way to meet Decker, she stuck her head in the lab. "His temp's jumped again."

"Damn it." Linda swiveled on her stool and jumped up. "We need those facilities and fast."

"On it." Emma ran for the front door. When her feet hit the bottom step, Decker raced up.

"What's wrong?"

She explained as quickly as possible what was happening and what they needed. His mouth pressed into a line. "Fucking hell. You do realize you've already been as exposed as you can get."

Shit. "Good point. We need to quarantine and move out quickly. I can take the doctor now so she can get started using the lab. Are there any vampires who have not been in proximity to this? We need blood samples from at least one."

Before he could respond, a commotion pulled them away. Two people approached, and neither looked well. Emma ran toward them as Linda raced down the stairs. They both reached the pair at the same time. One was a vampire, the other human. Both male. Did this mean something? It was too soon to tell. Before they were able to get the men inside, Jag appeared.

"Since demons have thus far been immune to plague, I'm here to portal you back."

Relief swept over Emma. "We have gurneys there if we need them."

"I bet you have an actual hospital too," Linda said putting her arm around the vampire to assist him.

"We do."

"And Ethan is still there keeping the place running," Decker added. "Since I'm already likely infected, I'll go with you." He went inside for Hunter while Jag opened a portal. It only took them seconds before they were all back in the familiar hall of site R.

"This way." Emma led Linda and the others to the infirmary where they quickly got their sick patients into beds.

"Emma, can you stay here while I go back and grab some things?"

"Yes, I'll get vitals on our new patients."

"Thanks. Jag, can you take me back?"

"Sure thing."

Jag and Linda left the room while Emma grabbed the items needed to check on the two newest patients.

"Can I help?" Decker asked.

"Sure, you can take vitals while I draw blood. How's that?" She started prepping vials for the newcomers.

"On it." He grabbed what he needed from the cabinets. "The supplies in here are getting low. I'll grab more from the storage later."

"Thanks. I hope we don't need them, but just in case." Emma had a bad feeling about this illness and prayed she was wrong. It appeared like a normal flu, but then again, the Red Death started like a cold until your heart exploded. She tried not to think about it and pushed herself into nurse mode. They had a real doctor now. Maybe they could finally get some answers.

DECKER COLLECTED the data Emma needed and by that time the doctor was back in the lab processing the blood. She'd also managed to collect a sample from what she hoped was not an infected vampire as well as a human. There had been people who'd not been near Hunter in several days. From what she'd said, she was looking to see if there were any differences in the samples. She might also learn if this was a normal flu.

He doubted it. Immortals didn't get sick and while unmated vampires were only close to being immortal, Decker now was thanks to mating Emma. He was also feeling like fucking death on two legs. He'd left the infirmary saying he was going for more supplies in the storeroom. Instead, he made a quick detour. First, he went to a nearby phone and dialed up Ethan, who he hoped was camped out in the monitoring room.

The geek picked up on the first ring.

"Yo."

"Yo? Listen, stay locked up in there if you can. I think we might have a new epidemic on our hands."

"Damn it. Okay. I've got enough supplies for a few days," he replied.

"Good. I'll stay in touch." He hung up, then headed outside. Stuck inside a mountain, he'd learned that his telepathic link had limits. Mainly, it didn't penetrate rock. Outside, he was able to contact Ryder and Shade.

Listen up, I'm feeling whatever this shit is. How are you guys?

So far, fine. However, we've got five more human males coming your way, Ryder replied.

Decker wiped sweat from his face. The ground swayed beneath him, and his vision slanted. He'd probably better get inside.

We also have some news, and it's not good, Shade interjected. *Jag found a faint scent of Morbus on the other side of the river. He says it's probably a couple of weeks old, but not old enough that whatever illness that demon left behind... It's likely still active.*

Fuck our lives. I gotta go before I fall over. They were never going to catch a break. He had to get back inside and tell the doc and Emma what he'd learned. This would be no normal flu and there would be no motherfucking cure.

They were screwed.

He made his way back in the heavy door and somehow managed to get into the main compound. Every step was like dragging a herd of elephants behind him. He leaned against the wall as a wave of nausea hit hard and fast. He vomited. His last meal of blood splatted the concrete floor until it looked like a crime scene. There was no standing. The pounding in his head so bad he wished for someone to tear the damn thing off.

Decker slid to the floor and laid his cheek on the cold, hard surface. He swore steam swirled upward he was so hot. He tried to will his body to move. No one would find him here as Jag was opening a portal further inside. Maybe Ethan would see him on one of his cameras. Maybe he would die here. His mind raced to Emma. They hadn't even started a life yet, and he was going to leave it. Wasn't that what he wanted? Not long ago he would have begged to join Sophie, but now he would give anything to stay. He realized he'd only been holding onto his past because he thought he owed a debt. His past hadn't wanted him back. His redemption was in his future, and now he was going to lose that too. It was in this moment of reflection that he realized he had somehow fallen in love with Emma. What a perfect fucking time to come to his senses. On his deathbed.

SOMETHING KEPT CRAWLING up Emma's spine, but it was more of a feeling than an actual thing. She tried to shake it off, but it refused to leave her. Her patients were resting as comfortable as possible, and the doctor was in the lab running tests. As she sorted through the supplies, she realized Decker hadn't come back yet.

Panic set in.

He was likely infected too. Was he sick somewhere? She ran to the lab. "You haven't seen Decker come back this way, have you?"

Linda looked up from her microscope. "Nope. You look concerned."

"I'm going to look for him. If you need me, pick up the phone and dial eight-three-three. It will turn on the intercom and you can page me."

"Got it."

"Any luck yet?"

Linda gave a sigh. "Nothing yet I'm afraid."

"I'm sure you'll find it." She prayed anyway and left the infirmary to look for her mate. In the corridor, she stopped and searched deep inside of her. She and Decker had a connection now, and it was time she learned to use it. Her gut told her to head toward the entrance and not the storeroom. What was he up to? As she ran to the elevator, she rounded the corner and stared into a scene from hell. Decker was face down on the floor, a pool of blood—or what appeared to be blood—was close by. He didn't seem to be bleeding so she assumed it was vomit like the other vampires since it was their main source of nourishment.

"Decker," she yelled as she rushed toward him. He tried to push himself up, but it was apparent he was weak. "Let me help you."

The second she touched his skin, she realized he was burning up. "We need to get you into the infirmary." She wrapped her arm around him and between the two of them, they were able to get him on his feet. "What are you doing on this side of the compound?"

"I wanted to let Ryder know I was infected. Jag is bringing more and the bad news is Morbus... there."

"What?" She shook her head as they started to walk. "Never mind, I'll talk to Jag when he gets here and find out what's going on. How bad do you feel?"

"Like complete hell, but I got this." And from somewhere, he mustered the strength to walk faster.

When they got to the infirmary, Linda and Jag were working on two new patients when suddenly one of the vampires they had brought in earlier started to convulse.

"Go," Decker said as he plopped himself onto an empty bed.

Both she and Linda reached the vampire at the same time. Linda shoved some bags of ice around the vampire. "You have actual ice here. You'll have to tell me later why you guys left. Start an IV, please."

Emma was already prepping his hand and prayed she still had the skill to get the needle into the vein. A thrashing patient made her job that much more difficult.

"Got it."

"Here, give him this." Linda handed Emma a syringe. "I hope these drugs work on vampires. I'm rolling the dice here and I don't like it."

"I know." Emma administered the drug, and they waited. It didn't take long before the seizing stopped and she took his temperature. "He's still a hundred and two. This makes no sense." His temperature wasn't high enough to cause a seizure, it had to be the illness itself.

Linda cast her a worried glance. "I definitely don't like this. Why the seizures? From what I've learned being with Shade and the other vampires is they no longer have any of their human illnesses." She looked at the other men who seemed to be resting. "And, are they next or is this only a symptom he's having?"

As soon as the question was out of her mouth, the vampire arched his back, his body stiffened and red foam excreted from the corners of his mouth. The monitors attached to him blared. He was in cardiac arrest.

"Damn it!" Linda yelled as she ran for more drugs. "You know what to do?"

"Yes." But while Emma was prepping, he flatlined. "Shit," she muttered and started CPR. Linda rushed in and assisted, but nothing was working.

I'm a damn witch, shouldn't I have some kind of power to save him? She prayed, wished and begged, but he wasn't coming back. After several minutes, it became obvious their attempts were futile.

"I need to call it," Linda's soft voice pulled Emma from her miserable thoughts.

She stopped the chest compressions and lifted her head. Her gaze met Decker's, and she realized there was every chance in the world that she might lose him. Things didn't make sense. How was she supposed to help him?

"Oh my god! Where did Jag go?" She needed that demon, stat!

CHAPTER NINETEEN

EMMA RACED DOWN THE CORRIDOR, boots slapping concrete the only desolate sound to be heard. Jag had gone back to their new camp and now she was cursing the fact he was able to open portals while she couldn't. Why was that? They both had magic. She was near panic when she ran into him as he came around a corner looking ragged.

"Emma, this thing is spreading and there are just too many to bring back here."

"Still only the males getting sick?"

"So far."

"We lost one. A vampire went into cardiac arrest and Decker's sick."

He offered a sympathetic look. "I know."

"No, you don't get it." She realized she'd grabbed the front of his shirt and was shaking him. Letting go, she smoothed the fabric. "Sorry."

"I get you're concerned."

"No. I mean yes, but the angel Eva told me I had to save my mate. Could she have meant this?" She started wringing her hands, then shoved them in the pocket of her jacket. She was about as nervous as one could get. The need to be next to Decker instead of out here talking to a demon was making her crazy.

"It's possible since he's mated his symptoms may not worsen."

"I can't take that chance. There has to be more to this. I mean, she also said humanity needed us."

Jag's gaze narrowed. "Emma, tell me word for word exactly what this angel said to you."

She shoved an annoying curl from her face. "I don't know. Something about I was chosen, he needed me."

This time he grabbed her shoulders and gave her a gentle shake. "No. Think. You have to recall her exact words. I need to know."

"Okay, okay!" She closed her eyes and thought about the beautiful angel who had spoken to her. "She said, 'You have been chosen, Emma. Your mate needs you, you need him and humanity needs you both.'"

He smiled. "Those sneaky angels." He grabbed her hand and started to drag her behind him. "Come on, we need to see the doc."

"Wait! What the hell's going on? What did she mean?" Here all along Emma thought it was to help Decker with the ghosts from his past. Had she been wrong about that?

"I think I know what she was trying to say. At least I hope so." They ran down the corridor and back into the infirmary where they nearly knocked Linda from her feet.

"Hunter's fever is spiking and his blood pressure is elevated," Linda whispered. "I'm fearful he will be next. The drugs aren't working."

"I think I know how to cure this," Jag said.

"I thought there were no cures for Morbus's plagues." Linda cast a weary look at their patients. "Decker seems to be doing the best so far, but I'm going to say that's because he's mated."

"We need to create a vaccine using Decker's and Emma's blood."

"Oh my god, that's perfect." Emma's excitement heightened as the realization of what Jag was saying set in. She started to gather supplies to extract blood.

"Wait." Linda halted her. "First off, it takes months of testing to create a vaccine and second, that is not my specialty."

The demon waved her off. "We have magic, two people chosen by higher powers to save humanity and a lab. It's perfect."

"Oh fuck it." Linda grabbed a band and motioned for Emma to take a seat. "We've got nothing else and in this strange new world, this just might work." A couple of minutes later, they had two vials of Emma's blood and two fresh ones from Decker who thankfully was sleeping.

Emma leaned over and kissed his forehead. "Hang on. You and I are going to fix this." She moved away and stopped at Hunter's bed, giving the vampire's hand a squeeze. "Don't stop fighting. I need you to hang on a little longer."

She looked over at the other patients who, so far, were not in dire straits. They needed to get this done and fast. She headed into the lab where Jag had donned a coat and took on the look of a mad scientist as he bent over a microscope.

"What can I do?" She glanced at Linda who sat on a stool at the end of the counter.

"Don't look at me, I'm just observing. Dr. Jekyll here is our residential expert."

Jag slipped a couple of vials into a centrifuge and turned it on. "In a few minutes, I'm going to need all your magic. Start thinking healing thoughts."

She chewed her lip. "I'm not sure how to do that. I mean, do I just think about healing?"

He cast her a glance, one brow jacked up. "It's not rocket science. Breathe out the bad and breathe in healing and calm. Think only of wellness."

"I'm new at this, okay?" She took in a breath, shook out her hands and closed her eyes. Emma wasn't sure what to visualize, but she thought about healing. About wellness, then the blue lights she was becoming so familiar with attacking the virus. It consumed it and left whole healthy cells behind it as it continued its work.

"You're doing something." Linda's voice filtered through. "Your hands are glowing blue."

"Now, Emma. Take these vials and dump that magic into them."

She opened her eyes to see Jag holding the vials in front of her. She took them and folded them into her palms, encasing them in the blue light that sparked from her fingertips. Again, she thought of the virus-attacking light. Of hope and healing and even tossed in a prayer to Gaia. The glass on the vials glowed for a moment as she felt power rip through her, and then the light was gone.

"Damn, I hope it worked." She was left fatigued and handed the vials back to Jag. "What now?"

"We make a test batch. Won't take long," he replied.

"Fine. I'll go check on the patients. I hope this works." She stood and left the room. The need to see Decker and make sure he was all right overwhelmed her. Back in the infirmary, she checked on the others first. Hunter was no better, but he wasn't any worse either. God, she prayed this vaccine worked. It was almost too much to hope for. She moved to Decker, who opened his eyes when she approached.

"Hey, how do you feel?" She touched his forehead. Still warm.

"Like shit, but at least my gut isn't rolling anymore."

"Really?" She took his temperature. It was down a degree. Was it possible he was recovering on his own? If what Jag had suggested about her and Decker being the answer to this plague, then it was possible. Her hopes grew. "Good news, your fever is down a little."

He started to sit up.

"Just what do you think you're doing?"

"Getting out of bed. I've got things to do. How many others are down?"

"A lot. So far only the men, but Jag is working on a vaccine." She went on to explain, and it was when he stopped her that she realized she had never told him about her encounter with the angel.

"Wait, you said Eva?"

"Yes."

"Pretty, dark skin and hair?"

"And white wings. What's going on?" She was getting the feeling he already knew her angel.

"She came to me back at the house. After you left. Told me she had sent you back and how she had been with Sophie when she passed."

Emma squeezed his hand but didn't say a word.

"Said Sophie was happy now, and I needed to move on with you."

"Wow. I get the feeling higher powers are at work here."

"Yeah, I think they are."

DECKER WAS ON HIS FEET. Still not fully recovered, but so much better than he had been hours ago. Seems his body took care of fighting whatever new, fucked-up plague Morbus was currently spreading. He stood over Hunter, a man who had been by his side on many missions both before the Red Death and after. Hunter was an excellent Navy Seal who had also lost his family to the plague. Hunter had survived though, and when he'd asked Decker to change him, it had been a no brainer. He had been Decker's first and neither of them knew what the hell they were doing. Hunter was a survivor, it seemed.

He watched the doctor insert the needle into the IV. This was the vaccine they all hoped would be their saving grace. A mixture of his and Emma's blood along with her magic. Hadn't the angels said he and Emma were to save humanity? Time to put that theory to the test, because if this didn't work, they were all screwed. It was only a matter of time before Morbus snuffed them all out.

"Hunter, you rotten fuck. Get better and out of that damn bed," he commanded, and Emma squeezed his hand.

"This will work. I'm sure of it."

"I hope you're right, otherwise it sounds like we may lose every man in camp." He looked at her. "That leaves you vulnerable and I don't like that one damn bit."

She smiled, but he could tell it wasn't full of confidence. "Careful, vampire. You keep acting like you care, I might start to think you do."

"If I didn't care, I would have never bonded with you, little witch."

"Decker." The look she gave him spoke volumes. "Finding you lying on the floor like that... Well, it—"

"Scared the ever-lovin' hell out of you?"

"Yeah, it did."

"I had the same thing happen to me when you were attacked. Matter of fact, every time you are out of my sight or when you're in my sight and a threat arises. Fuck, I worry all the damn time."

She let out a laugh. "Maybe we do care then. It's not something we've talked about since mating."

"Jesus fuck, can you take your mushy shit to someone else's bedside?"

They both gasped at the same time and looked down at his friend. "Hunter, glad to see you back. How you feeling?"

Emma had already sprang into action to take the vampire's vitals and the doctor—who had been administering the vaccine to the other patients in the ward—rushed back to his side.

"Like I've been to hell and back, but not nearly as bad as when you fucking changed me."

"His fever broke," Emma said.

"This is wonderful, but we need to see how the humans react to the drug. Could be an entirely different ball game. Vampires have a much faster metabolism. Hopefully, we'll have good news soon." Linda slung her stethoscope around her neck. "I need to find Jag so I can go back to the camp and check on the sick there."

"I'll stay here and watch over our patients."

Linda gave a nod, then was gone.

"Has anyone asked her about her marking?" Decker asked.

"No. So much has been going on since I met her, we haven't gotten a chance to have small talk. Ace showed any interest in her?" Emma focused on Hunter. "Since all your vitals are fine, it will be okay if you want to get up and wander around as long as you don't leave the compound yet. The doctor will need to release you for that."

Hunter wasted no time in tossing his covers aside and getting out of bed. "I hate hospitals," he mumbled as he tested his legs. "I'll be in the barracks taking a shower." And he was gone before either Emma or Decker could protest.

"He wastes no time. And to answer your question, I've not talked to Ace since we got back from retrieving Shade. I need to though." He needed to thank the vampire for being a stubborn dick and proving it was Decker who was Emma's mate.

"Decker!" Emma's excited voice pulled him from his thoughts. "We have another one awake and their fever has come down."

This was good news. Just maybe they could weather this storm.

EPILOGUE

FOUR WEEKS HAD PASSED, and everything was back to normal. As normal as it could be in this new world. The vaccine had been the success they needed and only one vampire had been lost. Decker had never been more relieved. The thought of leaving Emma alone haunted him on a daily basis. Apparently, he still had some ghosts to deal with.

The door opened to the small home he and Emma now shared, and she walked in, tossing her things to a chair.

"Hey, there. Did you guys have any luck locating Wolfe yet?" She walked to him and slung her arms around his neck.

He pulled her close. "Not a word. Ryder and I spent most of the day trying to plot different routes he might take. How did your day go?" He kissed her.

"Okay. Jag and I made some progress on mapping gates. We started drawing them out and marking where they go. He says once this is complete, we can gate jump and not have to worry about using a portal to try to get close."

He looked down at her. "Did you go through any of them?"

She grinned. "What if I did? I am a witch after all."

"I don't care. I need to be there to protect you. I refuse to back down on this matter."

"Hmm." Still grinning, she ran her fingers along his pecs. "There you go, sounding like you care again."

He caught her wrist. "That's because I do. You took all of my heart a long time ago." He claimed her mouth. Tried to show her with actions how much he'd grown to care. A blue electric pulse sizzled between them and it no longer concerned him. It was part of who Emma was now. A witch, and every day he watched her powers grow. Jag was right, Emma was going to hold immense magic one day and Decker would be there to help her.

He slipped his hands under her shirt and up her back. Her skin silky soft under his calloused fingers. He unhooked the one bra she saved for when she had to go out in public. He hated that thing and was going to make it his mission to find her some new lingerie. She deserved pretty things, and he was selfish. Wanting to see her clad in red satin and lace wasn't a bad thing, was it?

He suckled her neck, the spot he always drank from and the one that made her moan like she was now.

"You are such a tease."

"That was my goal so you would beg me to bring you release."

She looked up, black filled the brown in her eyes and she licked her lips. Her arousal was all around him, yet she pretended not to care.

"What if I don't beg, but say I have other things to do tonight?"

He stepped back and gave a shrug. "As you wish." It was hard not to grin when the look on her face changed from smug to panic.

"You're an ass."

He let out a laugh. "I thought we established that long ago."

Her sexy mouth curled into a wicked grin. "We did, vampire." She grabbed the hem of her shirt and pulled it over her head so slowly he thought he might age several years before she was done. "I think I'll do chores in my underwear."

"But you're not wearing a bra."

"Oh I'm not done yet." She kicked off her boots, then wiggled— with more hip action than was necessary—from her jeans and tossed them in a nearby chair. "Now I'm in my underwear."

"You're an evil witch."

She batted her lashes. "Why, whatever do you mean." She'd even dropped her voice into a low seductive inflection. His mate was good at this game, but he was not one to be outdone.

"I like your idea. It's refreshing." He stripped off his tee and tossed it with her jeans. He knew Emma better than she thought. She was a sucker for his hard abs and low-slung jeans.

She chewed her bottom lip. "God, did you look that good before you became a vampire?"

"Honestly? I worked my ass off to stay in shape. Being a Seal meant hard training. All the fucking time."

She sighed. "And now your delicious perfection is frozen in time. I give up." She moved faster than normal and slapped her palms on his chest. Started pushing. "To bed, mister."

"What if I don't feel like it?"

She pressed her breasts into his naked chest then cupped his cock. "Your erection says otherwise."

"Evil witch," he hissed, then wrapped his arms around her ass and tossed her over his shoulder. She never resisted as he moved to the bedroom and tossed her on the bed.

"Such a brute. Now—" she threw her arms over her head "— come fuck me."

Now that was a command he would never refuse. He shed his jeans then parted her thighs, positioning himself between them. The ache in his cock had him wanting to plunge deep inside her, but he wasn't done teasing her yet. He placed the tip at her entrance then gripped her hips, pressing her to the bed.

"Keep those arms up. You move and I stop, got it?"

Her pupils dilated further. "Yes."

He swirled his tongue around her nipple, teased her as she tried to arch into him, but he didn't allow her. His fangs dropped, aching to sink into her flesh so he could taste her and watch her come undone. He refrained, instead scraping the points over her breast and eliciting a shiver from his mate.

"You're going to torture me," she whispered.

"I'm a Seal, I've been known to do unsavory things to get what I want."

She wiggled her hips and managed to get the tip of his cock in, but that was all he allowed. It took every bit of reserve he had though not to seat himself balls deep. This woman was going to undo him if he wasn't careful, and he had every intention of bringing her to the edge so he could watch her fall.

"I'm not one of your conquests."

He responded by flicking his tongue over her nipple then giving a light bite.

She gasped, then moaned. "I'm going to die from sexual frustration."

He chuckled. "Lack of sex never killed anyone. Besides, you just had me this morning."

"Not enough," she muttered.

"I would tend to agree." His reserve now lost, he sank deep into her sex. Her warmth engulfed him and made him feel. Feel more things than the simple pleasure of sexual gratification. He was more his old self these days. Less on guard and able to relax when he and Emma were alone. A slap on his ass brought him back to reality.

"I told you, keep those hands over your head or I would stop."

"You can't stop now, you're too committed."

Damn, she was right, his little witch. "You know me so well." He grabbed her wrists and pinned them where he wanted them. "But I have ways off making you submit."

She bucked her hips.

He pulled out then thrust back in until he had a rhythm that left his mate gasping. When he had her on the edge, he kissed her neck then bit. Her taste filled his mouth and her screams of pleasure his ears. His bite was a sure way to send her into blissful orgasm over and over again until she was left begging him to stop. After three pulls of blood, he sealed the puncture, always careful to never take too much. He nuzzled her neck as his world exploded. He would never get enough of this female that fate had decided belonged to him.

∽∽∽∽∽

EMMA WATCHED the morning sun filter through the sheer curtains she'd managed to find. Their small house was starting to turn into a home. As much as it could without modern conveniences of electricity and plumbing. Several of the men had managed to build community showers and catch rain water. Shower time had to be limited to a schedule so they could make sure they had enough water. At least until someone figured out how to harness the town's wells. She never realized how much of their lives depended on electricity. Things had to go back to how the settlers lived.

She rolled onto a sleeping Decker's back and kissed his shoulder. Her life had changed so much and he had become a huge part of it.

"I hear your mind grinding away. What are you thinking about?" He rolled to face her.

She looked at the markings on their wrists. The ones that now matched and said they were bonded. Every day she felt him more. Knew where he was and that he was okay. He was the other half of her soul, but there was one thing she had yet to say.

"Does any of this seem real yet? Us, I mean."

"You're the only thing in this world that does."

"Do you think we made the right decision?"

He propped up on an elbow and arched a brow. "You having second thoughts? It's a little late, ya know. I'm not sure how you break a bond like this."

"I'm not but wondered if you are."

"No."

That was it? She stared at him for a moment, then rolled to her back. It wasn't long before he towered over her.

"What's up? Something is bothering you."

The bad thing about bonding, you tended to feel each other's moods. Not to mention, Decker was a walking lie detector. He knew when she was not being truthful.

"We've never talked about our feelings."

"And?" There went that brow again.

"I love you, thought you should know."

"I see. Well, thanks for telling me." He rolled to his back.

That was it? Did she care he didn't reciprocate? No, but she knew she lied to herself. Sitting up, she reached for her clothes. Maybe if she got busy with chores, she could forget this moment and pretend it didn't bother her.

"Emma?"

"Lots to do today." Work was never done in their new town, and they still needed to try out the gates. There was still hope of other survivors in the world. His fingers brushed her naked back, followed by a kiss.

She smiled and considered rolling back into bed when the alarm sounded outside.

"Fucking rogues," Decker muttered as he was on his feet with lightning speed, tossing weapons on the bed.

"We're never going to have peace, are we?" Emma dressed much faster these days. Magic was a big help in that department.

"Probably not." He pulled her to him and kissed her so deeply her knees nearly buckled. When he finally broke free, he whispered, "I love you, little witch. Stay alive for me."

There was no stopping her smile. "You too."

She would, and so would he. They were stronger and better together and they would continue to fight and keep those who survived safe. There was no way either of them would give up. Besides, a little angelic help really did go a long way.

ABOUT THE AUTHOR

Award winning and bestselling author Valerie Twombly grew up watching Dark Shadows over her mother's shoulder, and from there her love of the fanged creatures blossomed. Today, Valerie has decided to take her darker, sensual side and put it to paper. When she is not busy creating a world full of steamy, hot men and strong, seductive women, she juggles her time between a full-time job, hubby and her dog, in Northern IL. Valerie is a member of Romance Writers of America and Fantasy, Futuristic and Paranormal Romance Writers.

Sign up for Valerie's newsletter and be the first to hear about new releases, receive special excerpts and exclusive contests. http://valerietwombly.com/newsletter-sign/

Follow Valerie
www.valerietwombly.com

f facebook.com/FangedFantasy

y twitter.com/fangedfantasy

instagram.com/valerietwomblyauthor

BB bookbub.com/authors/valerie-twombly

ALSO BY VALERIE TWOMBLY

More books you may love, visit my website to view all my books.

Eternally Mated Series

Guardians Series

Sparks Of Desire Series

A Jinn's Seduction Series

Beyond The Mist Series

Demonic Desires Series

Dark Horizons Series

Lightning Source UK Ltd.
Milton Keynes UK
UKHW010629250520
363802UK00001B/159